Elizabeth Glaister

The Perfect Path

A novel. Part 1

Elizabeth Glaister

The Perfect Path
A novel. Part 1

ISBN/EAN: 9783337065706

Printed in Europe, USA, Canada, Australia, Japan

Cover: Foto ©Andreas Hilbeck / pixelio.de

More available books at **www.hansebooks.com**

BY

ELIZABETH GLAISTER

AUTHOR OF 'THE MARKHAMS OF OLLERTON' 'A DISCORD'
'A CONSTANT WOMAN' ETC.

'Enter the Path! There spring the healing streams
  Quenching all thirst! There bloom th' immortal flowers
Carpeting all the way with joy! There throng
  Swiftest and sweetest hours!'

E. ARNOLD, *Light of Asia*

IN TWO VOLUMES

VOL. I.

LONDON
SMITH, ELDER, & CO., 15 WATERLOO PLACE
1884

CONTENTS

OF

THE FIRST VOLUME.

———◦◦◦———

THE PERFECT PATH.

CHAPTER I.

SEEKING THE ROAD.

Aim high, strike high.—*Proverb.*

A NICE crisp roll came flying out of the dining-room window of the Hôtel des Citrons at Mentone. It flew with more force than precision, and hit the wrong man, who was a quiet invalid strolling down to the shore for his morning walk. It gave him a threefold shock —to his nerves, by smartly striking him on the ear; to his principles, that good food should be thus wasted; and to his feelings as an Englishman that a young countrywoman should so misconduct herself. The right man was not

VOL. I. 17   B

farther off than the distance between the feminine aim and hit. He understood at once, and, without apology to the wrong man, who sadly pursued his way, called out, ' Hulloo, Corks ! bad shot that. What the mischief are you after now ? '

A handsome tall girl, of about seventeen, leant out of the window and replied, ' I want you to walk with me. You have missed the train ; it is on the bridge already.'

' What a confounded nuisance ! What a scourge you are, Corks ! '

' Not a bit of it. I did not make you too late ; it is better for you not to go to-day, for you are horridly out of luck. I have missed you with the roll, which is one to you ; and I am going to take you for a walk, which is another.'

' Don't seem to see it ; you will scamper all over the district ; and I am tired. Can't walk in this hat either.'

' Put it in the hall ; I will bring you a soft

one and a white umbrella. You may have a donkey if you like—Montebello has his saddle on.'

' Tha-anks awf'lly, especially for the donkey; if I must go, I must, and would rather walk than have you and Mathilde running beside and whacking the poor beast.'

Mathilde, who passed by just now with a grave salutation to the gentleman, was one of the princesses of the Mentonese donkey-women —a beautiful, dignified woman, tall and straight, with a sad expression in her dark eyes, as of one who saw many follies pass by her which she would not join and could not prevent. She wore her country dress, perfectly neat and clean—a flat hat with broad black ribbons, and jacket, skirt, and apron of striped cotton, soft both in colour and texture. Hearing that the young lady did not want her this morning, she went on, leading her big brown donkey, who shook his large ears, and took life, without enthusiasm it is true, but calmly—for if Mathilde often called ' éza '—shame—upon him, her words were harder than her blows, and he was better off than most of the horses.

The slangy-looking young man, who so grudgingly accepted his friend's invitation to walk with her, was the Hon. George Kingdon, a person of high family and low fortune, who, having failed to qualify himself for a profession, was misspending his time on the Riviera by living at Mentone and going nearly every day to Monte Carlo ; it was the train to that place which he had just missed.

The girl who spoke to him was Cordelia, daughter of Lieut.-Colonel John Ashby, by his second marriage with Rosina, daughter of the late Henry Stafford, banker, of Maybury, Southshire. A young woman of such respectable lineage ought not to be found throwing a roll out of window at a young man bound to her by no ties of kindred, and behaving as if her conduct were of no consequence to any one. Mr. Kingdon would have been very angry if his sister had so acted; but he encouraged this poor Cordelia, and called her 'Corks' in the open street, for, in spite of respectable names, she was little respected. Her father was more constant at Monte Carlo, and at places where the pleasures of Monte Carlo were to be had, than George Kingdon himself, and was too frequently described as 'rather shady' or as 'a doubtful kind of bird.' Mrs. Lichfield, her half-sister, in whose charge Miss Ashby was at present, had nicknames too, and people wondered why Lichfield let her run about by herself while he was soldiering in India.

For part of the winter Mr. Kingdon had been one of Mrs. Lichfield's admirers; but now, in April, he was fallen into the second rank, partly superseded, partly retiring. He was not unhappy in his humbler position, and was nearly as often in the Ashbys' society as before. Cordelia amused him, and he made himself her friend, treating her as child or woman according to the fancy of the moment. Though quite without conspicuous virtues or any shining good qualities, he was a gentleman, in a feeble and ineffective sort of way, and acted up to the character in treating her as a child when they two were alone, and as a grown-up young lady only when he wished to plague Mrs. Lichfield, or to compel some one else into a show of respect for the neglected girl.

Probably nowhere in England, even at the quietest watering-place, would Mr. Kingdon have walked with Cordelia in her present guise —dusty boots, a rush hat with a piece of muslin round it, a fine, but shabby and not very clean, gown, and a faded red parasol with a bull-dog's head for the handle. Yet it was not so much her dress that made her look wild and unconventional, as her air—her way of walking and of looking about her. Though tall and well-built, with a firm round figure, she looked, not a woman, but a big child, with a child's freedom of step and glance, and a child's outward look,

the world and her surroundings being as yet
more interesting to her than herself and her
relation to them.

Her companion did not study her, nor
greatly care what she looked like here in Mentone, where, after the manner of his kind, he
despised all who were not English as foreigners,
or distinguished but to curse the too obtrusive
German. He did not know, nor would it have
disturbed him to know, that the stately but not
more discriminating Mentonese class all the visitors together as ' *les étrangers* '—convenient as a
source of income, but inexplicable and not worth
explaining; probably mad, and certainly heathen.
He did not care, for he was still rather sulky
at having lost his train, and yet not entirely unwilling to be led off to the hills by Cordelia, and
to give up his proposed amusement altogether
for one day. So he tramped morosely for the
first dusty mile by the sea, where the beauties
of nature are chiefly hidden behind and beyond
high walls; but when they turned under the

olives on the hill behind Roccabruna, he resumed his usual mood of apparent good nature and real indifference to all but his own present pleasure, which made him ready to be amused, and to enjoy the rare combination of sunshine just warm enough and shade just thick enough which is found under olive-trees in spring on the Riviera, and is one of the chief delights of the choice time and place. He found a comfortable seat, and began to smoke; Cordelia went on a quest for flowers, and found none— for violets and anemones were over, and the gladiolus and cistus not yet out; a great yellow snapdragon was all her reward, and presently she came to sit down by her companion.

'I am glad you lost your train, George. The Colonel is not going to-day; he has not been since the day he dropped so much— Sunday, was it? His temper is really too nasty, I should have had to stand it all the morning; as it is, I shall not see him till dinner-time, and Sophy will have to take her share.'

'She is much more in the line of filial duty
than you are.'

'Yes. If she vexed the Colonel, *he* might
have a fit of duty, take her to Worthing, and
settle her there with me and a highly recommended governess, which Duncan Lichfield—
bless his innocence!—believes to be the case
at this identical minute.'

'That would be rather rough on your
sister.'

'Wouldn't it? Rather different from driving to Monte Carlo, with Lord Twiston in the
carriage, and Major Spires, or perhaps you, on
the back seat with the Colonel; then a little
dinner after, and perhaps a round game, with
pretty gowns and nice complexions, and all the
rest of it! Fancy Sophy at Worthing, sitting
in a nice damp place on the sand, with her
hair gone soft, minding baby—the darling, he
would like it!—and knowing all the time that
the highly recommended's off eye was on her
from the bow-window of the lodgings; and

might be, for all the mischief there was to get into ! '

'And you, Corks, how would it suit you?'

'Down to the ground, George,' answered the girl, looking at him with the utmost gravity and earnestness. 'Of course, the work and the deportment, and the punctuality and order, and the highly recommended generally, would be huge nuisances ; but life can't be all beer and skittles.'

'Have you found that out? You must have been reflecting deeply.'

'People who make their lives like that do not come to much. You are all for beer and skittles, George ; and, unless you pull up very short, you will never be much.'

'That is what my people say, putting it rather differently. Who knows, however, if *you* take to moralising? A good deal depends on how " much " you want me to be.'

'You do not want to be anything yourself, you know. I do ; I should like to be something very particular, and that is why I wish Sophy had tried Duncan's plan. It would be hateful; but I hope I can bear disagreeable things when they are really necessary.'

'Hurrah for Corks, the heroine! You are coming out in a new light, my cherished child.'

'Look at me here; do you suppose I do not know how badly I am treated, and cannot guess how the money goes? Do you think it is nice to have this queer gown, and to feel Madame Villemain sneer, and see Baldy and Beaky turn up their eyes—their sort of nose won't turn up, but they feel like it? Do you think it is sweet to be growing up a ragamuffin, and knowing nothing in particular, nearly eighteen that I am?'

'You are growing into a very nice-looking girl, which is worth something I should say. No one wants you to pass exams., nor earn an honest living, nor be a credit to your family. I think it must be fine to be you, Corks.'

'That is all you know about it. I ought to

be exactly different. I like you, George, and it is quite awfully too good of you to chum with me as you do; but if I were brought up like your sisters, you would not tell me I was nice-looking, nor call me Corks.' This was said with the utmost pathos, and Mr. Kingdon took his cigar out of his mouth and looked out to sea before he answered.

'My sisters are not in the least nice-looking; their names are Lavinia and Isabel, and I never heard that they had anything so jolly as a nick-name between them. It would not amuse them at all to be chummy with me.'

'Ah! you know what I mean. If I had gowns like Sophy's, and went to Monte Carlo when I liked, and not only for a dummy; and if I rode anything better than Montebello and Grisette, and had some music lessons, and money to spend at Rumpelmayer's, it might be rather jolly here; but that is not what I really want.'

'You seem to have morbid longings for

respectability, a backboard, and a German
governess. I have none of them to give you,
unluckily; but if you could moderate your
desires to a gamble, or a pound of *marrons
glacés*, something might be done.'

'It is not respectability that I want—Baldy
and Beaky would give me that any morning for
the asking; nor the governess either, unless
she were of a sort; but at Worthing one might
have a chance——'

'Out with it, old woman; I cannot bear
suspense. What is this mysterious need of your
being, that neither I, nor a Fräulein, nor the
Misses Greenley can satisfy? Do you burn to
marry a marquis, or a chimney-sweeper?'

She was sufficiently afraid of ridicule; her
desire was very deep in her heart, so deep that
it did not often trouble her, though she was
usually conscious of it, but to-day it had
pushed up to the surface. George Kingdon
was only moderately sympathetic, yet her
desire to tell some one, just to hear how it

would sound aloud, was so strong as to overcome all minor considerations.

'I want to be really very good; not
respectable, or just proper and the right
thing—but real strong goodness, the very true
best kind.'

George tried his best; he did not wish to
hurt the girl's odd, sensitive, unexpected feelings, so he struggled; but the idea of old Greyleg Ashby's daughter, the sweet Sophy's sister,
his friend Corks, aiming at exalted goodness,
was too much for him. He looked at the
figure by his side—the indescribable cut of her
gown, which he justly suspected of being an
old one of the Sophy's, the exaggerated frizzle
of her hair, the irreconcilable cock of her
rush hat, the bad style of her generally, taken
with the quickly coming beauty of her handsome child's face—and he failed, he leant back
against the olive trunk, and laughed long and
loud.

Cordelia was a little hurt—not much, for she

was not used to be considered, and she looked
for something like this from George. Tears
came into her eyes for a moment, but she
turned her face away, and they were gone
before George had recovered his composure.

'My dear child! My poor old Corks!
What has brought you to this? Who has
been filling your venerable head with these
notions? It is all a lot of narrow-minded
rubbish, you know, and it won't do at all, for
it is not your line, and there is no greater
mistake than taking up anything not in your
line. It is not the way of any of your people,
unless it be your brother-in-law?'

'I do not think Duncan's way of being
good will suit me: he is very rummy; but
I do not know—I had not thought of it when
he went to India.'

'You will have to alter pretty considerably
before you join the truly pious. May I be
there to see?'

'No, you won't, if I know it. I do not

want to be pious, or to go about converting people, or anything like that. I mean something quite different. I do not think there is any name for it.'

'How will you set to work? There were some revival folks about here lately. Is it a Moody and Sankey turn, or will you join the Salvation Army, and hop backwards before a lot of roughs, singing hymns at the stretch of your voice? That will take some breath, and I don't see that I can help you. Besides, it is very bad form, you know, and will not improve your position with the Colonel or Mrs. Lichfield.'

George laughed again, but he looked suspiciously at Cordelia. Girls left to run as wild as she did were always getting into scrapes and making queer acquaintances. Some low fellow had been canting and palavering to the child. He—George—would spoke his wheel for him, and that without delay.

'Of course I could not begin here, or by

myself, and I may have to wait ages long before I find any one to teach me.'

'I thought shepherds always lurked in ambush to devour stray sheep. I wonder very much whose crook is round your leg now. Come, my Corks, make a clean breast of it; who has been trying to convert you? I do not deny that you might be better, but I want to know who is going to improve you.'

'No one! Oh, George! I have told no one but you!'

'That is taking the first step in the right direction.'

'Don't you see, it is not just behaving pretty that I mean, nor doing anything—but that sort of goodness from inside that a very few people have. They do not do anything particular, but they are stronger and nicer, really better than anybody else; it just shines out of them.'

'Precious rare folks, I should say; not many running about this wicked world.'

'No, that is just it—there are so very few;
but I should like to be one of them. I have
seen some, or I should not believe in them any
more than you do.'

'Where are these wonderful people? Have
you seen any here?'

'No; there is little chance in our set.'

'I think that was a parson you hit this
morning with the roll. Did you mean gently
to hint that he might find a convert at the
Hôtel des Citrons?'

'Next time I want you I will howl out
your name into the street; you will like that
better. There are some parsons good in the
way I mean, but I do not know them. There
was Mary Morton, our washerwoman's mother,
at Weymouth; but she could not teach me,
dear old soul! The best person I know is
Sœur Lucie at the convent school I was at in
Brussels. I wish I was with her again; but
the man who does my grandfather Stafford's
business was down on the Colonel for sending

me to the convent. He was an owl to interfere in the wrong place! I wonder if he
knows that the governess never came with us
here.'

'Did they try to convert you at the convent? I believe that for a foolish thing and
making a general muddle of your prospects
in life there is nothing like turning Roman
Catholic. Don't meddle with that. Plymouth
Brethren and Moody and Sankey are frightfully
low form, but they do not land you in such a
pickle with your belongings as the Romans do,
and people are much oftener cured of it.'

'I cannot do anything now. Some girls
look to being soon married, or to being pro-
digiously run after, or very rich. I have seen
some who went in for being very learned, or very
High Church, or nursing, or being great guns
over botany and beetles, or dab hands at draw-
ing and painting. Those things do not make
people nice, and lots of dummies go in for
them all. I mean to go in for being good.'

'And what is to become of me? Are you going to cut me and leave me out in the cold, or do you mean to convert me too when you are satisfied with yourself?'

'That would be best; only you will have to make up your mind and go in for it steadily. When I find some one of the right sort to put me in the way, I will tell you; only you must promise not to tell any one, nor to plague me. I am sorry now that I told you.'

'You need not be sorry, old woman. Now let it be a bargain and fair doings. I promise not to say a word, nor chaff you; and you promise to tell me when you find a patron saint to your liking and begin your holy career.'

'Very well, I promise. I have a roll in my pocket; will you have half?'

'Thanks, no. Eat it yourself, unless you want it to shy at somebody.'

'I wish I had the other now; I am s‹

hungry. Let us go round the hill and into the Gorbio valley. There is a path most of the way, and I want to get some irises.'

'You are a rum sort of girl, Corks. I wonder what you will grow up like.'

CHAPTER II.

A WANDERER.

False blood to false blood joined.—Shakespeare.

ABOUT half a mile from the country town of
Maybury in Southshire stands a pretty house
known as Ivy Cottage. Its chief architectural
feature is a verandah, pleasantly suggestive of a
sunny situation ; the garden speaks of sunshine
too—the whole is faultlessly neat, and looks as
if a comfortable income were spent there. It is
only partially screened from the high road, and
passers-by catch a commonplace but agreeable
glimpse of easy, peaceful, and wholesome life
within. And it is life, if of a gentle and unex-
citing type, that is to be found at Ivy Cottage,
though what the tradespeople call ' the family '
only consists of one old lady, her maids and
her man, her one fat dog, and her two tyrannical

Angora cats. One spring morning this old lady, Miss Hooper, stood just within her gate waiting for some one to pass by. She was a gentlewoman clearly, though of a very plain and unornamented pattern ; a square simplicity expressed her habits of mind and life—floridness and elaboration were needless to her, she had nothing to hide and nothing to pretend to. She was rather short of stature, solid rather than stout ; she had a bright complexion, and very bright eyes ; her cap-ribbons were bright too, and her dark grey hair made crisp curls all round her wide forehead. Her head, held upright, expressed great energy ; but her figure looked stiff and immovable, for she was lame, and only walked slowly and with the aid of a stick ; to come from the house, through the flower-garden and by the little carriage drive to the gate, about one hundred yards in all, was the extent of her walking powers. She looked along the road in the opposite direction from the town, and presently saw what she had come to see—Mrs. Wastel, of Wastel Warren, in her old bonnet and grey shawl, walking with a majestic and highly trained air along the liberal greensward that borders the road, holding up her gown with one hand and carrying a tin pail in the other. This is a woman of middle age, tall and graceful, with a fair face still; gentle and thoughtful, she looks wise with a pure and guileless wisdom, and though she has known both sorrow and joy, it is plain that she has never entered into any hard and vulgar conflict of life—she has the outward look that comes of inward peace and the total absence of selfish aims and self-conscious struggles. She is Miss Hooper's niece, and she smiles with pleasure at the old lady's greeting.

'I thought you would be coming down about this time, Julia, as it is the day for the district meeting. It is a long walk for you.'

'Yes; but Lettice is going to Lee this afternoon, so I must e'en trudge. Mayne's cart will pick me up on its way from the station. I have special business at this meeting, and Dinah Bowling's soup ——'

Miss Hooper was usually ready to plunge into poor-people talk, but something else was in her mind to-day. 'Julia, I have sent for Rosina's child.' The younger lady forgot her benevolences and drew nearer the gate.

'Have you, Aunt Susan! Is not that more kind than wise? Will not a child trouble you, to say no more?'

'You are young enough to know how the years go. I thought of a child, too; but yesterday was Rosina's birthday, and in thinking of her I counted that this girl must be nearly eighteen. As it was wet, and no one came to keep me out of mischief, by post time I had written to that man, and asked for her to visit me. Ever since I have been doubting, and waiting for you to come and call me a foolish old woman.'

'Perhaps too kind an old woman. If the burden come, we must share it with you. I

hope that man will be civil to you. Poor
Rosina! How much this gives one to think of.'

Mrs. Wastel's eyes grew sad; very rare
tears were in Miss Hooper's.

'Poor Rosina! How we loved her, and
what shipwreck she made! Julia, though she
is dead, dead fifteen years, I am never sure that
I fully forgive her. Shameful is the only word
for her marriage, and I am sore and angry still
when I think of it.'

'Yes, it hurts us still; but I am sure you
forgive, or your kind old heart would not go
out a-wandering after her daughter.'

'Perhaps it is only a wilful going in search
of trouble, and a throwing away of the peace
of these last years. Suppose she is like her
mother; she may be, and it would be too
much to go through all again.'

'If only she be not like her father!'

This was putting into words Miss Hooper's
secret dread. For forty-nine years of her life
the 'wicked man' of her devotions had been

vague, abstract or varying; but for the last
nineteen years he had become concrete, acquired
a distinct personality, and stood in the shoes of
Colonel John Ashby, her late niece's husband.
She made a comical, yet piteous, face at her
friend—this other niece, who was so much
better than Rosina, so entirely rejoiced in and
approved, yet hardly so dear.

' Never mind, Aunt Susan; a girl of eighteen
will not put us all to the rout. We at the
Warren are as much bound to her as you are,
and she shall be made over to us should she
prove too much for you and the old maids.'

Said Mrs. Wastel presently to Mr. Odiarne,
the Vicar of Maybury, ' Aunt Susan is in a little
trouble, Philip.   Shall you see her soon?'

' I was there on Monday; I will look in this
evening, instead of Merridew.'

Miss Hooper and the Maybury clergy made
pets of each other. It was not easy to say
why she should be on a different footing with
them from the other parish old ladies, but she

was. This favouritism had gone on for years,
and though Ivy Cottage was now more of a
second clergy-house than ever, owing to Miss
Hooper's strong delight in her present vicar, no
one ever found it of any use to be jealous of
her. She was the loyal motherly friend of one
generation after another of curates ; any well-
conditioned young man found it a pleasure to
be favoured by the kindly old lady—so shrewd,
sensible, and full of fun, and so ready to bear
the burden of any trouble they might bring to
her. Religious talk was seldom heard there,
for Miss Hooper was full of shy, old-fashioned
reserve on things dearest to her; but there was
a quiet confidence that the foundations were all
right, that gave a mingled firmness and liberty
for all that was said to or before her.

Just now the Maybury clerical staff consisted
only of two curates, though sometimes there
were three. Of these two, Mr. Knox, the senior,
was a dry, practical little man, upright and
severe, carrying terrors for the ungodly, and

not generally known to be extremely tender-hearted and to cherish the pathetic romance of a hopeless engagement. The junior, Mr. Merridew, was a bright-faced, happy young creature; rather embarrassed by his high spirits and sense of the ridiculous, and much afraid of being thought frivolous. Mr. Odiarne being unmarried, the body of divines lived at the Vicarage, composing what Miss Hooper called a rough-and-tumble household, bestowing on it her sincere but needless pity.

After Mrs. Wastel's hint, it was not long before Mr. Odiarne went to Ivy Cottage. It is not easy to describe this Vicar, for descriptions convey the idea of quite an ordinary kind of clergyman, and he was not ordinary. Mrs. Stepney, a clever flippant sort of person among the neighbours, said that he was like a chapter in the Bible, having a simple quaint sweetness at first reading, and when read by simple folk, but that scholars and students found him to be full of occult learning, deep meanings, and

varied interpretations. He was very thin and
unusually tall, very straight and upright; this
fine carriage did not prepare people to find him
gentle and absent in manner, and rather reluc-
tant in speech. His face was straight and firm,
with features a little small for his height, his
complexion was dark, and his hair and short
whiskers were at this time of an iron-grey
colour. To those who saw him day by day, he
appeared as a quiet, hard-working, and not
very popular parson; he owed the last defect
to being quite unable to make a fuss about
people, and a very marked dislike to being
made a fuss about; but he was never fully
seen or known but in his preaching—then his
eyes flashed, and his speech was free, his great
powers of mind had full play, his strong, deep
enthusiasm burned and glowed, and his eloquence was the hot overflow of his full heart.

'Can you speak like that to an unsympa-
thetic audience?' asked a brother cleric of
him one day after a sermon, during which the

strong excitement of the congregation had been very apparent.

'I do not know; I do not remember ever to have had one,' was the innocent reply.

Mr. Odiarne was not related to Miss Hooper, but he knew her before he came to Maybury, eight years ago, and he followed the habit of his cousins, the Wastels, and called her ' Aunt Susan,' which pleased her well.

'I have not heard much of these Ashbys,' he said, when Miss Hooper told him of her rash act of invitation.

'No; one speaks little of people whose very name is hard to utter. My sister Mrs. Stafford had but one child, and as she died when her baby was quite young, I thought the more of the little one that was left to me. My father was living then—an invalid, helpless rather than old—and little Rosina was the brightest and dearest thing in our lives. Julia Wastel was the daughter of my half-brother, who lived in London, and she was in no way

dependent on us, or needing motherly care, as
Rosina did. We were living in the old house
then, Red Place; and you know where Henry
Stafford lived—in the Marchmont's house, a
very good house—the bedrooms are excellent.
We saw the child every day, and in her
holidays she stayed entirely with us, and Julia
came too. Rosina was Julia's chosen friend;
and though we all spoilt her, I think Julia's
devotion was the most spoiling of all, for
she was older, steadier, cleverer, and much
better brought up. It was the child's beauty
that bewitched us all!'

'You, Aunt Susan, who have quite a pre-
judice against good-looking people!'

'I am going to tell you why. We idolised
that girl—her father and mine, Julia and I, we
were all alike. We admired her going out and
her coming in, her little naughtinesses, as well
as her affectionate ways; every new gown that
she had we conveyed to her that it was she
who adorned it; every other girl we found her

inferior, and we let her see that we did so. She was very pretty, a lovely child, a graceful, dancing, winning creature, full of frolic and pretty, unexpected ways. She was full of little rebellions, too, and would play at all sorts of pranks, sure of our forgiveness. We treated a downright disobedience no more severely than a bit of mischief, and did not make enough of the little deceits and playful deceptions by which she got her own way. At the time, all this seemed but pardonable weakness, and the indulgence needed to make the life of a motherless girl as happy as possible; now I know that it was sin. Worst of all in me, for Julia was young herself, and had a girl's generous infatuation for her younger, prettier, and more brilliant cousin; Henry Stafford was much engaged and troubled with his business— he had no other joy, and a man, too—but I might have known better; in me it was sin, blind and selfish sin!'

'You have repented it long ago; I cannot

allow you vain regrets,' said Mr. Odiarne, gravely.

Miss Hooper's vigorous old head bent a moment from its upright carriage, and she was silent for a space.

'It must have been a butterfly nature—she could not have had much character; we made her selfish, and did not look for her faults; but she must have had little feeling, and certainly no principle.'

'I do not yet know her fault; but in such a life she would have been little tried, and have learnt no self-government in the school of experience. You know that ideas of right and wrong can hardly be called principles till they have had many trials.'

'I know that an old maid like me is not fit to bring up a child; and you, Philip Odiarne— well, a man is of no use when a pretty girl, child or woman, is in question! But you were not there, so you need not look ashamed. Ah! she knew nothing of self-denial, self-restraint—and we did not teach her. God forgive us!

'In those days there was a good deal of society about Maybury, of a kind that has passed away now; it was pleasant for the young people, and I used often to take Rosina out, with and without her father. A Major Ashby was often seen about Maybury in the hunting season, sometimes at the inn, and sometimes in lodgings, when he had his wife and child with him, and on his long leave. They were rackety, ultra-fashionable people, not of our sort. The wife's behaviour was not what was then thought becoming in a married woman, though the husband was much quieter. He was very handsome, and had good manners; he was more of a man of fashion than most of Rosina's partners, but being at least forty, and married, we saw no reason against her dancing with him occasionally. She would say she liked him better than the young men, of whom she had plenty of choice; but that seemed only

a little coquettish air, and she made friends
with the child in the street, though I do not
think she knew the wife.   Another winter this
Ashby spent his leave with the Maystons, of
Stone House, bachelor brothers of no good
reputation.   He was alone, and it was known
that Mrs. Ashby had left her husband; there
was a divorce, and the child was in the father's
charge.   Of course, this was not much spoken
of before Rosina, but she knew quite well that
Mrs. Ashby was not dead.   Ashby was not at
the dances that winter; we met him in the
town sometimes, but he merely bowed; and it
occurred to none of us that Rosina could have
any further acquaintance with a gentleman
staying at Stone House, and not known to her
father.

    'One day some one said significantly to
Henry that Miss Stafford seemed to enjoy her
walks in the Birch Piece with Major Ashby.
You know that the garden of that house opens
on the Birch Piece, which was very little fre-

quented before the new bridge was built; and
Rosina used to come that way by herself to
see us, though she never walked alone through
the town or into the country. Henry was ter-
ribly vexed, and scolded everybody but Rosina.
She told him a lie, and partly satisfied him;
but in a few days he went to the Birch Piece
himself, and met the two strolling together
as if it were quite a habit. Ashby was very
cool, and rather insolent. He said he was now
free, and wished to marry Rosina; but we have
always thought that he had only been diverting
himself, and calculated on her father's complete refusal. Henry could not bear to see
Rosina's tears, and she persuaded him to take
the matter seriously, and make some inquiries
about Ashby. It was a pity—if he had been
sent about his business at once, there would
have been a speedy end so far as he was
concerned, and Rosina would not have died
of a little fretting—or so we thought, too
late.'

'Ah! we have most of us plenty of after-wisdom,' said the listening Vicar.

'Ashby was bitterly angry with Henry for asking about him, and vowed vengeance, which to be sure he took. We heard nothing good of him; apart from the divorce, which was obstacle enough for us, and the fact that he had been courting the child before he was free, he was a known gambler, and had exchanged from his late regiment under doubtful circumstances; he had many debts, no prospects, and very little property; and it was broadly hinted that more care and attention might have saved his wife from her ruin. It was out of the question that he should be engaged to Rosina, and she was told so with all care and tenderness, and even apologies, from us all. Julia was sent for to be with her, and a foreign tour was planned; but at the end of a fortnight, when I, an old fool, began to think she was resigning herself, she ran away with that man, and none of us ever saw her again.'

'Poor girl, poor girl!' murmured the Vicar.

'Rather say, her poor father!' exclaimed Miss Hooper, briskly; however far astray her own sympathies might go, she desired to find her pastor's in the right place. 'I will not speak of myself, we grow used to our burdens; but Henry's grief was terrible; most of all he felt her deceit and the lies she had told. It was her heartlessness that hurt Julia and me the most. Even my father took it greatly to heart; we thought him past caring; but his last days, otherwise so peaceful, were all clouded by the wrong-doing of our darling. Julia was married in that same summer and came to Wastel Warren. We thought very highly of your uncle, and he was so devoted to and suited to Julia, that we could not regret his being a good deal older and having a son already to inherit his property. She was very happy, but we were all so cast down and bereaved that we could hardly take comfort in Julia's joy.'

'And Mrs. Ashby?'

'She was married—if that can be called marriage—to some horrid foreigner, and has lived abroad. Oh! you mean Rosina. She never wrote; she never asked forgiveness; she died and made no sign, three years after she left us, when her second child was born; it died too. We think Major Ashby meant her to be reconciled to her father, because of the money; but he hated Henry, and so put it off too long, deluding her with false hopes: this we gathered from his letters at the time of Rosina's death. For her, the only thing that showed she thought of us again is that she named her girl Cordelia, after her own mother, my sister. That is not much to go upon, for we were all proud of the old family my mother came of, and from which we got the name.'

'In this sort of case you must pick up all the crumbs. She probably repented sorely, and, we may hope, fully.'

'I sometimes think that if she had fallen

into a well the day before Henry heard of her acquaintance with Ashby what a saint we should have made of her, and what a gentle tender regret we should have felt.'

'Ah! the saints are the tried ones, only we do not always see it! Is that all your story?'

'So far as such a story is ever all told. Henry Stafford died a few years after Rosina. He was a true brother to me, and more in my life than Oliver—Julia's father. He lived in hope of reconciliation with Rosina; and when her death deprived him of that, he made no fight in his last illness, and died of what I thought very insufficient bodily cause. He was not rich, apart from his earnings, and he left his property to his brother—except about two hundred and fifty pounds a year to Mr. Horley, his partner, for the benefit of Rosina's child. It is more than strictly tied up, for it is that good Horley's own; he is only bound, as an honest man, to use it for this girl's benefit; yet Major —he is now Colonel—Ashby contrives to give

him a great deal of trouble about it. It was
a suspicion of Horley's that the girl did not
have all the good that she ought to have from
the sum he at present allows that decided me
to ask her here.'

Miss Hooper ended with a heavy sigh, as
much of foreboding as of the pain of retrospect.

'She may be a comfort to you yet, dear
Aunt Susan. We will see that she is not too
much of a torment.'

'Thank you. Julia says the same; but I
must not pull down a load on my own shoulders
and then cry to all the world for help.'

CHAPTER III.

AN OPENING.

She spoke, and, lo ! her loveliness
Methought she damaged with her tongue.

Jean Ingelow.

ONE day, not long after Cordelia's last walk
with George Kingdon, Colonel Ashby was dis-
covered to be in a very bad temper. This was
not so rare as to excite much surprise, and
he was the more vexed because his younger
daughter took no notice of his disturbed state.
She was feeling lonely, dissatisfied, and embarrassed with herself. Mentone was growing
very hot; she had walked a long way in the
morning, and was tired—she who professed to
be untireable; and she had provoked a battle-
royal with the Misses Greenley, and got ruffled in
it—she who professed to care nothing for their
opinions and denouncements. The elder and

invalid Miss Greenley was the more aggressively pious and overbearingly religious of the two sisters. She had a formidable hook-nose, wore a very fierce cap, and was always ready to do battle with the open sinner or the Romanist, whom she regarded as being on a pretty equal and very low level, as regarded their prospects in the life to come ; she was in the habit of explaining this with great vigour of expression and freedom of outlook. Her sister, who was her constant nurse, seconder, and *souffre-douleur*, was milder, smaller, and tamer, both in aspect and speech ; she looked as if she would have had delicate health, had not Miss Greenley begun first, and so acquired a prior claim to care and consideration. She wore no cap, though the space between the two sides of her hair was a ' parting ' indeed, fully two inches wide.

The places of these ladies at the table of the Hôtel des Citrons were next to the Ashbys ; opposite sat a Pole, who possessed all the talents for conversation with ladies—pretty ones—that so eminently distinguish his nation. Unused to the freedom enjoyed by English girls, he found Cordelia a delightful novelty. The fun between them was often fast and furious; and Cordelia, on this occasion, stayed in the dining-room to enjoy it after Mrs. Lichfield, who never flirted noisily, nor across the table, had finished her luncheon and gone upstairs. Goaded and scandalised by this behaviour, Miss Greenley expressed an opinion that Cordelia was a reprobate, and required much praying for.

'I beg you will not think of it, Miss Greenley. I suppose it is possible you might succeed, and I am sure I do not want the things that you would ask for,' was the flippant answer.

'Oh, my dear! Augusta's prayers are a treasure indeed,' remonstrated Miss Amelia.

'I should not mind yours so much, Miss Amelia, though I am afraid you would like to see me a very damp, spooney kind of creature ; but I must firmly decline Miss Greenley's.'

'You know not what you cast away,' pleaded Miss Amelia.

'Yes, I do. My family would be truly grieved if they were answered. Have you ever seriously sat down to consider how deep they would be in the waters of affliction if I were to turn goody-goody on their hands! Picture my aged parent's despair! I might even come to think it wrong to quarrel with my daily omelette !'

Cordelia retired victorious, to the joy of the Pole ; for Miss Greenley had just given the landlord, the secretary, and three of the waiters a very poor time about the omelettes served at luncheon.

In their little *salon* on the first floor sat Colonel Ashby and Mrs. Lichfield, in peace and amity, till Cordelia came. Colonel Ashby was a very handsome man, tall and well made, with a broad smooth forehead, and dark hair turning grey in a becoming manner: thinner than formerly, but still showing as much inclination to curl as was compatible with patrician fineness and delicacy of growth. His whiskers curled in the same discreet manner, and under his small moustache was seen a mouth that always smiled. He was chiefly terrible when this fixed smile did not accord with his feelings at the moment, and had to be contradicted by the imperative bend of his nose, the uplifting of his well-marked eyebrows, and the flash of his dark eyes. These eyes were handsome in themselves, but their setting sloped too much downward at the outer corners to be in keeping with the Colonel's broad forehead and constant smile.

Mrs. Lichfield was smaller, fairer, and with less accented features than might have been expected from her father's daughter; but she resembled him in her smile, and in the peculiar setting of her eyes. Her pretty head was covered with admirably arranged little curls;

her gown was fresh and lately put on, and she so far respected it that her little son of three years old was made to play at a safe distance from her.

Fergus was a little fair child, grave and thin. He loved ' Cordie ' better than any one in the world, and made for her directly she came in. Thérèse, his French nurse, was constantly kind and devoted to him, as French nurses usually are; but she teased him, and screamed at him, and never let him amuse himself in his own way. Only Cordie understood him—she allowed him to play with her as he liked best ; she provoked the slow sweet laughs that did not come if he were hurried or frightened ; and she, who was a proverb for being careless of what she said or did, was unfailing in her tact and patience with the one creature that at this time she really loved. It was necessary that the boy should play quietly when Colonel Ashby was there, so Cordelia kept a private treasure of home-made toys in her pocket for him; and it was a little store of champagne corks, begged from the waiters for his benefit, that, being one day untimely brought to light, earned for her the name of ' Corks,' by which she was known to a limited, but not very select, circle of young men, of whom the Hon. George Kingdon was the chief.

Mrs. Lichfield was clever with her needle, and industrious too; with help from Thérèse, and the devotion of her forenoons, she kept her own wardrobe in a high state of efficiency, con-sidering the small amount of help she had from the leaders of the millinery profession— for her husband had very narrow-minded views about bills. She was busy now with some minor arrangement of frills and ribbon that absorbed her a good deal. Colonel Ashby was also understood to have his occupations, though what they were was not very plain He was not at all an early riser, and the care of his person occupied much time; he was often heard to express great disgust at the uncivilised habits of persons who could dress in less than two hours. The hotel luncheon was quite unsuited to his tastes ; he had only just left his room, and was taking his *déjeûner* and reading his letters.

Only Cordelia had nothing to do; she dawdled listlessly into the room, thinking that to be impertinent to Miss Greenley was but poor sport, and yet there was no better to be had till after dinner, when she was to act in a comic charade with the Longford boys, the Pole, and two American ladies who were staying at the Hôtel des Citrons. She wished her father good-morning, without much attention to or from him, cast a contemptuous glance at her sister, that included her toilette, her work, and her general character, in one concise depreciation, and sat down on the floor to play with her nephew.

'Cannot you keep that child quiet, Cordelia?'

'Cordelia, shut that window! Oh dear, will you never learn to manage the bolt?'

'I will do it, papa,' said Mrs. Lichfield, turning her head that way.

'On no account, my dear; do not rise.'

Colonel Ashby was always scrupulously polite to his married daughter; he was often floridly complimentary to other ladies—only to Cordelia was he ever rude or purposely disagreeable. He closed the window sharply, treading on and breaking some of Fergus's toys as he went.

'Naughty Colonel!' whispered the child— he was not allowed to say 'Grandpapa;' Colonel Ashby did not like it. Cordelia stifled the remark and turned the boy's attention to something else; the shielding of Fero was the only domestic duty that she recognised.

'Cordelia, get up! Do not sprawl on the floor like that!'

This personal remark aroused her to the perception that her father was seriously out of

E 2

temper, he so seldom noticed anything she did or said. The sense of danger woke her courage to meet it. She got up from the floor and seated herself in one of the hot and dusty velvet chairs with which the Hôtel des Citrons furnished its second-best rooms, and waited for the storm.

'How ungracefully you sit, and how heated and unladylike you look. You never look like a gentlewoman; I wish you were more like Sophy.'

'Do you! It would be very expensive to look like Sophy—pins, you know, and little things from the hairdresser, and real new gowns, for even her old ones do not make me look very like her; if it were not that my waist is inches and inches smaller I could not wear them at all,' said Cordelia, affecting to look critically at her gown. It was of pale blue stuff, and suited its present wearer very well, only it was a little short and tight, and missed the silver buttons, lace, and manifold etceteras that had helped it to adorn the fair Sophy.

'Cordelia is getting really too uppish and pert; nothing I do for her satisfies her. I wish you would consider that plan for her, papa,' said Mrs. Lichfield, who never entered into a war of words with her sister, and seldom found fault with her, but was stung now by the unkind reference to her waist.

'What plan? Are we to go to Worthing?' asked Cordelia, pleasantly excited.

'Worthing? Who is to know what may happen before Goodwood? What nonsense you talk! Goodwood, indeed, and Croxton Park hardly over!' The Colonel was pardon-ably irritated, and drank his claret and pushed his letters about before he spoke again.

'A relative of your mother—a Miss Hooper, in fact—writes to ask you to visit her.'

'Aunt Susie! Does she really? To stay with her? Oh, how screamingly jolly of her!' said Cordelia, springing to her feet.

'You think so, do you? I wish you may like it, on trial.'

'I am sure to like Aunt Susie; she loved mamma, perhaps she will love me.' Cordelia was quite off her balance; she spoke excitedly, and as her father seldom heard her. He promptly checked her inclination to sentiment by saying in his most supercilious manner,—

'Doubtless she will love you. Old maids usually require some outlet for their sympathies, and I remember Miss Hooper as a person of many superfluous emotions. One of them must have dictated this letter, though it is not in itself effusive. It will probably appear that her cat is dead, or has escaped from her fond care, as her pets have done before this.'

'Will you show me her letter?'

'Certainly. I cannot recommend it as a model of style; it is a little dry.'

'Miss Hooper presents her compliments to Colonel Ashby. She will esteem it a favour if he will allow his daughter Cordelia, her great-niece, to pay her a visit of some duration. Miss Hooper will be happy to receive Miss Ashby at any time during the coming summer.'

Ivy Cottage, Maybury.

' How deliciously kind of her! I call this truly sweet. Fancy a whole summer in the real country in England! I suppose I may go?'

' You must ask your sister; you are under her charge, though your relative has not the common politeness to refer to her. One must not expect much *savoir-vivre* at Maybury; your very existence is a proof of that.'

Mrs. Lichfield kindly spoke without further asking.

' If we had not Cordelia we could afford to stay a little in Paris after Aix-les-Bains; it would be a great gain to be without her at Trouville this year, it is bad enough to be obliged to take Fero.'

Hearing himself referred to in his mother's dispassionate equal tones, Fero threw himself across his aunt's knee and pensively kicked up his legs. 'My darling! If only I could take you with me! But I must go.' Then aloud, 'Sophy's consent is of just the same consequence as her care of me. We can live without each other for a time. Anything must be better than playing this eternal second-fiddle-out-of-tune at every hot watering-place in France. I should like best to go to board at the convent at Brussels, but as I suppose I may not, I should like to go to Aunt Susie.'

'I do not know where you learnt to be such an affectionate niece. It is very fine for you to talk of visits here and visits there, but you do not consider the expense to me. That cad Horley, who makes such an intolerable fuss about the shabby pittance he has to dole out, stopped your going to the convent—far the most reasonable place of tuition that could be found for you, and it is not likely that he will advance anything for your expenses in England, though it is well known to be the most expensive country in Europe.'

'If there is only a shabby pittance, perhaps he cannot,' said Cordelia, despondingly; this money difficulty in the way of her pleasures she knew was never got over.

'Did you suppose you were an heiress? Look here, a shabby hundred and fifty is all that can be screwed out of Horley; though there is more, which he says he is keeping till you come of age—the fool, as if it would be of any use to me then! He cannot be made to see that capital is frequently advanced for the education of a minor.'

'I thought Mr. Horley wished me to have a governess.'

'A governess! Really, Cordelia, you are too childish. Can you understand this—your expenses at this hotel, merely for your living, are not less than fourteen pounds a month; that is at the rate of a hundred and sixty-eight pounds a year. If your income is only a hundred and fifty, how do you suppose I am to provide governesses—a hundred and seventy for hotel expenses only, not to mention the daily, the innumerable, calls on my purse for your other requirements.' Colonel Ashby waved his hand largely, as knowing how great these requirements were. If he had not named them he might have quenched Cordelia, who felt weak in the presence of his arithmetic; but she clearly knew that her appointments were spare, rarely new, and only obtained at the cost of a fierce wrangle, and also that to have occasionally 'a half-day donkey' was the only personal luxury she ever attained to. He pushed his worm too far, and she turned.

'I do not know about the cost of living—I do not choose anything for myself; but I do know that I am kept very close and shabby, and have nothing nice as other girls have. If I go to Aunt Susan I shall not cost fourteen pounds a month.'

'That is why I mean you to go there. Your mother's friends ought to take their share. I do not know what Miss Hooper's income may be, but in mere justice half of it should be mine; she has no one dependent on her. You are, even for your age, so singularly devoid of tact that you are not likely to induce her to leave you your — or rather my — rightful share.'

'I can ask her if you wish; but I must go there to do it, and I must have some decent clothes to go in, and money to buy them.'

'No more impertinence, if you please; you have entirely spoilt my enjoyment of my breakfast, and seriously vexed me. I have explained to you the state of my affairs as few parents would condescend to do, and you immediately propose to squander more money in dress. Consult your sister about your clothes, as you are pleased to call them, instead of annoying me about trifles. If you have any ladylike instincts they will tell you that simplicity of attire best becomes a girl in the schoolroom.'

'That is just what I am not, and as I am nearly eighteen the schoolroom must make haste or it will not hold me, any more than Sophy's gowns.'

Then Colonel Ashby swore at his younger daughter, which she pretended she did not mind, and he closed the discussion by going out, leaving her to get over her excitement as she could.

'I wish you would not vex papa; he will be out of sorts all day,' said Mrs. Lichfield, in a tone that Cordelia thought beneath the gravity of the occasion.

'Why should he not be vexed? I wish I could vex him, really, thoroughly—not a little miff of a temper that he will get over by to-morrow, but a good rousing up, so that he will see that I am going to the dogs and do some-thing to stop it.'

'Don't be silly, you are to go to this old lady;

why can't you be content? I will see about your clothes. There is that white cashmere——'

'Sophy! you are worse than papa—much worse; he is only selfish and wants to be let alone and have no expense; but you are a thorough cat, always after some secret scheme of your own. I know why you want to have me done cheap and on the quiet this summer. I know who is going to Trouville. Some day you will wish you had let me go to school, or have a governess, instead of leaving me with nothing to do but to study you and your little ways. When Duncan proposed that you should stay with us at Worthing this winter, he meant it for kindness to me, and I shall not forget it.'

'Nonsense! Duncan has nothing to do with it, and I do not suppose he ever thought of you,' said Mrs. Lichfield, speaking lightly, but quailing.

'I shall write to Aunt Susan myself; then papa can say what he likes, and it won't matter,' pronounced Cordelia.

CHAPTER IV.

A DAMSEL ERRANT.

> Night by night
> He and his monstrous rout are heard to howl
> Like stabled wolves, or tigers at their prey,
> Doing abhorred rites to Hecate
> In their obscured haunts of inmost bowers.
> Yet have they many baits, and guileful spells,
> To inveigle and invite th' unwary sense
> Of them that pass unweeting by the way.
> *Milton.*

CORDELIA's letter was a work of time and thought, during which there was a cessation of hostilities, for, being less ready with her pen than with her tongue, the trials of composition subdued her for the moment.

'Sophy, are there two *n's* in "affectionate"?'

'Yes—at least, I am not sure; don't you know that it is always written short?'

'I am not sure how to write it short, so I have put it all as far as the *n*. I think there must be two; there are two in French, I know.

Her letter finished, Cordelia sat by the window gazing at the triangles of intense blue sea that were visible between the roofs of the neighbouring villas. Mrs. Lichfield thought she was getting over her temper-storm quickly as usual, and that she was herself showing much tact by leaving her alone. But Cordelia was like the lion of primitive natural history, who has a claw at the end of his tail, and when he wants to get into a rage he has only to wag the tail vigorously, and the claw works him up to the required pitch. Her claw, which she was just now digging fiercely into her sides, was the idea of her dead mother of whom she thought so much and knew so little, an idea always painfully excited by a quarrel with her father.

She knew that her mother was beautiful, because she was reproached for not being like her, and she knew that her life had not been happy, for who could be happy with Colonel Ashby; and then he spoke of her in terms of indifference or contempt; he plainly respected more that first wife who had the courage to show him how cheaply she held him, than the feebler and better woman who had weakly allowed him to break her heart. Something of the runaway match, and of the grieved and insulted father, Cordelia had gleaned, she did not know how. Of the moderate legacy left to her at secondhand she heard more, for Colonel Ashby never restrained his wrath on account of any feelings his daughter might have. Of Miss Hooper she knew but one thing. Among the few things in her possession that once belonged to her mother was a small manual of prayers that had accompanied the luckless Rosina in her flight; there was written in it, in a smaller and lighter edition of the same hand that was seen in the letter in Cordelia's lap, ' Rosina Stafford, from her loving aunt Susie.'

On these words, Rosina's daughter—so poor where her mother had been so rich—built castles enough, whole romances of love and forgiveness, reams of imaginary correspondence, and thrilling scenes of reconciliation. Now her heart swelled high—surely her castles had not been built entirely in the air, for they were founded on the old incorruptible stone of Love. 'Aunt Susie' was living and loving still, those stiff words of invitation proved it abundantly. Then those prayers were good, Aunt Susie must have wished her mother to be good—perhaps knew about it and would teach her!

But this full heart was also a very sore one. Colonel Ashby's taunts and scoldings were added to the old grievance of her mother's trials and supposed wrongs. Mrs. Lichfield's indifference and selfishness struck with fresh force against Cordelia's vehement wishes and tumultuous hopes; while over all was the sharp, bitter feeling that she was neglected and defrauded, allowed, as she said, to go to the dogs. To this store of explosives George Kingdon unwittingly set a match.

'How do you do, Mrs. Lichfield. Where is the Colonel? Has he gone to Monte Carlo? This is an off-day with me, and I hoped to find him at home.'

'Ah, Mr. Kingdon! You are doubly welcome, for we are dull this afternoon. My father is going to dine with Count Morlaix, and that is absolutely worse than Monte Carlo —he will be ruined, and without the music.'

'Let us hope he will ruin the Count. What are you doing this evening?'

'The other Count and Major Spires are coming to meet the Warlingtons and Mrs. Marish here for tea, and a little loo, or a roll of the ball. I would have asked you, but I thought you would certainly be at Count Morlaix's. Come; though you are too lucky at roulette.'

'Only at yours, I do not win many of the Blanc dollars. Hullo, Corks! What's up?

Hot face, red eyes, a dagger-and-bowl expression, an ink-smudge on your nose! You don't mean to say that some one has been rash enough to try to teach you to write! It has been hard times for that poor chap, I know.'

Cordelia's chin went up, but she did not speak.

'Do not tease her, Mr. Kingdon; she has been a little disturbed this afternoon. A relation of hers has asked her for a visit, and this impetuous child wanted to be off at once, without consideration of ways and means, while my father saw that there was much to consider. We do not care to part with her for an indefinite time, and, besides, are not quite sure that these relatives are desirable people for her to be very intimate with; I fancy my father chose the flower of the family. You see we treat you as a friend, Mr. Kingdon, and lay open our little discussion to you.'

Cordelia rose up in her wrath and blazed upon them. 'Have you done, Sophy? Would you like to say any more to George, who knows us all quite well enough to understand? I will tell him. George, the little discussion was a furious quarrel. Papa is in a diabolical temper, and so am I; we have said the most atrocious things to each other; he was the worst, because I was afraid to say all the things I thought of, so I have said them to Sophy, who always keeps her temper at the expense of other people's. They both want to get rid of me—Papa for cheapness, only it goes against him to please me and my aunt too; and Sophy wants me to go at any price—well, for reasons of her own; and both of them grudge the money to fit me out respectably—so there!'

'Come, come, draw it mild; you must take it easier than this,' said George, feebly. He was going to say 'old girl,' but felt that Cordelia was at too high a strain for that choice epithet to please her; and 'Corks' being open to the same objection, his appeal fell rather flat for want of a personal address.

'Don't be silly, Cordie,' said Sophy, with mild gravity. 'The money is a very secondary consideration, though it is not always easy to find it exactly when it is wanted, and Papa likes to give it spontaneously rather than to be asked for it. You must disguise yourself, and try to win a fortune at Monte Carlo; must she not, Mr. Kingdon?' she finished playfully, as one who would jest and turn to other matters.

'Very well; you have said it, and I will go,' said Cordelia, in accents of passionate despair, rushing out of the room.

'Poor little Cordie! she is quite upset; please excuse her, Mr. Kingdon; it is not often she is so uncontrolled, though she is always a little difficult to manage. Now sit down, I have not seen you for so long; have you any news, or the least little titbit of scandal even? You hear everything.

George sat down near the window, but he found that he could not command the terrace, and presently he forgot to look out, and gave

himself up to the enjoyment of a quiet half-hour
with pretty Mrs. Lichfield, who knew so well
how to make it pass agreeably. At the end of
it he asked, ' Do you know where your sister
is ? '

' No ; she went away in a pet, poor child,
fancying we teased her. I dare say she is upstairs, playing with my little Turk.'

' I rather think she went out. Is it possible
that she has fulfilled her threat, and gone to
Monte Carlo ? '

' Oh, no ! surely not ! She could never be
so very naughty.'

' She looked rather hot, you know ; and
when my friend Corks threatens a thing it is
not fear that keeps her off it.'

' But this would be outrageous. Perhaps
she is at Rumpelmayer's ; she is so fond of sweet
things, tiresome girl.'

Mrs. Lichfield sent upstairs to ask for Miss
Ashby. She had gone out in haste, half an
hour before, reported Thérèse.

'I am a little uneasy, Mrs. Lichfield; may I go and look for her? Had she any money?'

'No. Stay—yes, twenty francs; Papa gave it to her yesterday for some boots, and I know she has not spent it.'

'Well, I will ask at Rumpelmayer's, and look about the gardens. If I do not see her I will hop over yonder; it can do no harm, and if she has been so lively as to go I will take care of her. Say nothing to the Colonel.'

Mr. Kingdon did not trouble himself to go to the confectioner's, nor even to the promenade, but went direct to the station. A word with an official confirmed his belief that Cordelia had carried out her threat, and he presently followed her, grumbling to himself for the first time at the miscellaneous company carried by the afternoon train to Monte Carlo.

Of much less mixed character, tending to pure badness, was the assortment of people who arrived from Nice and overtook Mr. Kingdon as, after a search in the gardens, hoping that

Cordelia might have lacked courage to go farther, he entered the Casino. He knew that most of them were worse than they looked, and that even the most wilful girl of Cordelia's kind would be quite unable to appreciate them. He went through the hall, the reading-room, the theatre, all the loitering places, unsuccessfully, but in the first gaming-room, in the thick of that unholy fight, at one of the roulette tables, was Cordelia Ashby, sitting between an old Russian gentleman and one of the croupiers. Her eyes and her cheeks burned with the excitement of the afternoon, and from the hot and nauseous atmosphere of the crowded gas-lit rooms. In spite of the eagerness with which she was pursuing her end, she was playing with the utmost gravity and propriety, with full knowledge of what she was about, so that she was attracting very little attention from the players about the table, and it was past the hour for moralising sightseers. George judged it better to leave her alone for the present, for she did not look as if she would be amenable to any hint from him.

The gambler's fever was too strong in this young man to allow him to be a quiet watcher. Standing a little beyond Cordelia on the same side of the table, where he could give an occasional look to her, he began to play on his own account. At first he staked as she did, half with the gambler's superstition that such a player must win, and half in curiosity, to see if she won or lost. The crowd increasing, he could not always see what she did, and he used his own judgment in the intervals; then an unusual run of the numbers attracted his attention, for he knew not how long; when he next looked for her she was gone.

Cordelia's start in life was made with a piece of twenty francs. As she dashed out of the hotel, she calculated that this would give her four chances at one of the 'silver tables'; but the disadvantage of going through the world in a passion was brought home to her at the

station, where she must break into her first five
francs for her fare. She was known at the
Casino, where she had often been with her
sister, and, being tall enough to be by courtesy
twenty-one, she passed into the gaming-rooms
with the fatal facility extended to all who are
likely to hesitate for want of it. The evening
trains had not yet come in, and there was no
great crowd about the tables when she went in,
and she soon slipped into a seat, as being at the
moment a refuge from the more conspicuous
position of standing behind the chairs. The
croupier saw that this girl with the three big
silver coins for her capital was probably a runaway, and he kept his eye on her and made her
first transactions easy. Many games for half-
francs and coppers in the private rooms of
the hotel had made her quite familiar with the
board, and she had also been frequently in the
rooms and watched the players, though she had
not been allowed to play herself. Thus she
was not particularly nervous, and quietly made

her stakes on some of the even chances, losing
her first venture, winning the second and third,
and losing again the fourth. Then she waited
for two turns and began again, winning on the
whole until she got some gold pieces; with
these she played more boldly, and with varying
fortune, never quite coming up to the standard
of the two hundred francs which she had set
herself to win, and several times sinking within
her original capital. Once she lost it all, and
was on the point of getting up when the old
Russian, her neighbour, who had also been
watching her, said carelessly in English, ' You
have not the small money. Take then—take,'
and pushed two five-franc pieces towards her.
With a great increase of heart-beating on finding that she was observed, she took them
and staked them separately, losing the first and
winning with the second. She turned hot and
cold with fright over the last, remembering
that if she lost she could not pay, and this was
not like a party of penny roulette among

friends; but she won, paid her debt, took
breath, and went on again with fresh courage,
or rather fresh excitement.

It was just then that George Kingdon came
in and saw her. Time flies fast on darkest
vans over those tables; the crowd grew thick
about them, and many honest people who were
only touching pitch with one finger, when they
saw Cordelia's glowing face watching the
hopping ball, said, ' That is quite a girl; what a
shame to let her sit there with all that scum
about her! Has she no friends? Well, perhaps
she is as bad as the others,'—and so on. The
' scum ' had their word with the rest. ' These
English, they would be so proper, and they
allow a *jeune personne* to do thus.' There were
some also who said, ' By Jove! this is coming
it rather strong. Where is the Sophy?' and
' Old Greyleg Ashby is getting the filly in
training early.' Cordelia only knew that the
oppression of so many people standing round
her and leaning over her chair was becoming

intolerable. She began to stake rather wildly, and one lucky choice of numbers bringing her gains up to the ten gold pieces that she wanted, she slipped them into her glove, put down the surplus at random, won again, and got up, her head swimming. 'Ah, miss! go not now when your chance begins,' whispered the Russian.

'No, I have enough; good-night,' she returned, as she struggled out of the crowd, leaving her neighbour to a profound amazement.

CHAPTER V.

BY MOONLIGHT.

> O where else
> Shall I inform my unacquainted feet
> In the blind mazes of this tangled wood?
> *Milton.*

WHEN Cordelia came out of the Casino, the gleaming uncertain lights, the number of people passing up and down the steps, and the carriages with shouting drivers giving cracks like pistol-shots to their whips, bewildered her a little, and the first breath of the fresh night air made her giddy; but she ran down through the moonlit gardens to the station, where the full waiting-room and the aspect of the throng thoroughly frightened her, and for the first time! What horrible people! How dreadful to be alone among them! They are all looking at her, and —dreadful thought!—what shall she do when the train comes? A man spoke to her, another laughed in her face and completed her dismay. Looking helplessly round, she saw a French couple, of not very distinguished people, who were staying at the Hôtel des Citrons; she hardly was acquainted with them, and had chiefly noticed them to make a mock of their oddities; but now she thought a familiar face must needs be a friendly one, and going up to Madame Garvon, she asked if she would be so good as to allow her to go back to Mentone with her. The Frenchwoman made an indescribable movement of aversion and contempt, and screeched loudly, 'Impossible, Mademoiselle—impossible! Si vous trouvez à l'hôtel que je ne suis bon que pour rire, ici——' But her scornful laugh and gesture were enough; Cordelia turned and fled out of the station, along the road, up the hill, as fast as anger and fear would carry her.

She was hardly out of sight, and the laughter that pursued her had scarcely died

away, when George Kingdon came into the
station and looked round for her. He too saw
Madame Garvon, and, in despair, asked her if
she had seen Miss Ashby. She flatly denied
it, though she was still shaking with the excitement and triumph of her successful snub to
her English foe. 'It was, then, with Monsieur
that the demoiselle had come—not alone, as she
had been told!' Between vexation at himself
for having named Cordelia, and wrath at the
cold-blooded Frenchwoman and her malicious
looks, George swore aloud, which pleased her
much, for though she had often read of the
English 'big, big D,' it had never reached her
ears before. He was leaving the station to
seek once more at the Casino, when Madame's
little husband, a person of no consideration,
yet apparently not without human kindness,
touched his arm and whispered that Mademoiselle, his sister, had set off on the Mentone
road, 'bien vite!'

Without staying to bless after his banning,

and furiously angry with all the world, Mr. Kingdon followed Cordelia on the way pointed out to him, the carriage road to Mentone. The coolness and comparative silence when he had passed the first villas calmed him a little. It is not very easy, even for a strong person, such as he was not, to keep up a good hot rage and to walk fast uphill at the same time ; presently, too, he saw Cordelia skimming along before him, and the near success of his pursuit helped to bring him to a passable state of mind. How fast she had gone ! She could not have had more than three minutes' start of him, and she was already far up the winding road that leads away from the Eden-like valley, where the coiled glittering snake lies at the bottom. The moon lighted the whole semicircle of mountain cliffs and garden slopes; the trees cast deep shadows here and there across the white road, and Cordelia passed quickly through ' ebon and ivory.' At last she stood to gather breath under a great carob-tree, thinking she should

VOL. I.   G

be hidden in the blackness of the shadow; but her gown being of some very pale and shining blue stuff, she only carried a streak of moonlight into the shade of the dense old tree. She took off her hat, and looked about her, chiefly over the sea, as people naturally do when it is in sight—seeking the infinite, perhaps. She did not notice George, who, for his part, harmonised well enough with the shadow. The moonlight touched the olives on Cap St. Martin, but left the fir-trees black; the little waves washed white against the rocks; the bay was smooth, and dark with a soft and living darkness, and beyond it the open sea spread wide in a shining plain. A few red sparks and a deeper dusk showed where old Roccabruna holds aloof on her pinnacle from the sparkling new world at her feet; the woods crept up the hill-sides like the waves of another sea; Turbia, like a dead queen, lay on her lofty couch; and, above all, the mountains rose calm and high, their tenderest dusk just touched with softest light.

Cordelia, cooling her glowing cheeks in the soft wind, looked wistfully round on all this beauty, not ignoring it so much as deferring her joy in it. 'It is lovely,' she thought. 'Some day, when I am very good, I shall care more for it, I suppose, and want nothing more to make me glad. Now I only long for something that is not here.'

'Do you mean to walk home, Miss Ashby ?'

'Oh, George! did you come after me?'

'I think so, rather! What are we to do? Will you turn back with me and see if we can get a carriage?'

'No ; nothing shall induce me to go down there again—ever again. I must walk back : I am afraid it will be a long way for you. Your voice sounds as if you were in a jolly good rage with me ; and yet, I suppose, you mean to see me home.'

'It is three miles from here to the Hôtel des Citrons. Walking will be the best now, as we have come so far, if you are up to it.'

'I am quite up to it—and about the rage?'

'It is a good sizeable one, I assure you, my young friend; but it is not all for you, and I am not going to scold you now. Come, we must step out.'

They walked together in silence at a good steady tramp. When they met any one or were overtaken by carriages returning from Monte Carlo, and, above all, when they came to the dark places of which dark stories are told, where the olives close over the road with fantastic, uncertain shadows that seem to move though there is no wind to stir the trees, then she is glad of her companion and walks nearer to him. For his part he does not mind the shadows, but cares a good deal about the carriages. Cordelia has such a noticeable figure, and this moonlight is so clear! He does not as a rule care much for the opinion of people in general, and this unwonted exception is telling the more upon him.

'How much have you won?' he asks sharply.

'I do not quite know. I have it here; I can count. Two hundred and eighty-five francs.'

'Will that be enough for your gowns?'

'Yes, I think so'—in a very small voice.

'I hope they will wear well. I know women think all the world of their clothes; but I did not think you would have run such a rig as this for a little finery. What will you do when you are thirty, and dress begins to matter to your looks, if you go such lengths for it now when you do not want it?'

'It was not that, George. You do not understand. It was because I was mad with Papa and wanted to spite Sophy—they ought to have given me the money!'

'Oh! I am glad you have such praiseworthy reasons. I hope you are satisfied now. You have put your foot in it deeper than you seem to appreciate.'

' I was dreadfully frightened.'

' I am very glad to hear it.'

As they came into the western bay of
Mentone, the silence of the hotels and pensions
all so decorously shut up and with hardly a
light to be seen was rather appalling ; it gave
such a dead-of-night feeling, though it was not
yet eleven o'clock.

' Will the " Citrons " be open, or shall we
have to rouse the house and call the landlord
out of bed ? ' asked George, gloomily.

' The Colonel is out to-night ; he is always
very late at Count Morlaix's.   Max will be up ;
but I am afraid the door will be locked.   Some
of Sophy's people may be still in our *salon.*'

' Then I shall have a word with her.   Will
she be in a great worry about you ? '

' She will be disappointed that I am not
gone altogether.   Papa would not miss me for
at least a week, and when he noticed I was
gone he would say it was just like my want of
savoir-vivre.'

' Poor old Corks! '

' Don't, George! '

Max let them in discreetly. Max was the
head-waiter of the Hôtel des Citrons, an unfor-
tunate with such a white face, set off by such
very black eyes and hair, that he suggested a
snow man finished off with soot. Fortunately
he had so wide an experience of the queer
ways of ' *les étrangers* ' that nothing could well
surprise him.

On the first landing, George said, ' You had
better go upstairs at once. I will tell your
sister you have come in. Good-night, and
don't do it again.'

Cordelia began to thank him, but suddenly
burst into tears, and ran off towards her lofty
abode without another word. In Mrs. Lichfield's *salon* George found three ladies, seven
gentlemen, and a good many bottles. He declined a seat at the table where one of the
party was holding a roulette-table for the rest,
and going to the refreshment tray filled for

himself a sparkling bowl, while Mrs. Lichfield came airily up to him.

'Well, did you find that naughty child? I am afraid you have had a great deal of trouble.'

He felt that love had indeed grown cold as he answered in a low voice and a tone of infinite contempt—

'I found your young sister sitting in the gambling-hell down yonder by herself, playing at one of the tables, among a lot of the delectable people that are to be seen there of an evening—you know the sort, Mrs. Lichfield, though she does not. It will be all over Mentone to-morrow before breakfast. There are not many who know as I do that it is no fault of her own that she runs wild and uncared for, and has the chance of such doings as this. I warn you that I will not hear her blamed without saying what I know to excuse her. No, I can't say what you are to do about it'— in answer to an eloquent little gesture. 'Now you had better send the poor child some supper; she has eaten nothing since luncheon.'

Mr. Kingdon went away, leaving Mrs. Lichfield disturbed enough at last; but Cordelia got no supper, and sobbed herself to sleep alone.

CHAPTER VI.

SURVEYING THE GROUND.

*. . . Glancing all at once as keenly at her,
As careful robins eye the delver's toil.*

Tennyson.

'Dearest Aunt Susie,—Thanks tremendously for asking me to stay with you, and I am coming in spite of everything. I do not know when, for it is a long way, and it is not certain if we go to Aix-les-Bains. They won't let me travel by myself for the look of the thing; but I am coming. I suppose the Colonel will write to you; and I am out of my wits with joy. Receive my respectful compliments.

'Your most affectionnate niece,

'Cordelia Ashby.'

'Colonel Ashby presents his compliments to Miss Hooper; he is happy to accede to her request that his younger daughter should visit her. Miss Ashby will arrive at Maybury so soon as a fitting escort can be arranged for her.'

'Humph!' said Miss Hooper, comparing these notes. 'They should be shaken in a bag to make one good, honest letter between them. Plenty of compliments! Where has that child learnt to say "Aunt Susie," I wonder. She must come up in the omnibus, fitting escort and all, if they give me no more notice than this.'

Accordingly, one afternoon, at the end of May, the omnibus deposited at the gate of Ivy Cottage a tall young woman in a tumbled gown and the before-mentioned rush hat. She carried a large fan, but had no other travelling baggage. She bestowed a rapturous hug on Miss Hooper, who was not accustomed to be kissed, and did not like the practice.

'My dear, you are very welcome. If we had known you were coming, a servant should have met you with a carriage.'

When Miss Hooper said 'we' she meant herself and her maids, of whom she had five: a thin and aged waiting-woman,—no one ever called French a lady's-maid—a stout and aged cook, and a housemaid not much more than middle-aged. These three were the nominal strength of the establishment, but Cook was too old for much work, so her niece waited on her and did anything that required exertion; while Mrs. French, whose sight was impaired, had a young cousin to perform the same good offices for her.

'Dearest dear Aunt Susie, how perfectly lovely it is to come here!'

'Are you alone, my dear? And your luggage?'

'My portmanteau got itself lost at the junction. I told all the railway people to send it on, or it would be curious for them. Yes, I am alone; the Colonel does not do escort duty. Sophy is too yellow to be seen after her passage; and as to Thérèse, she thinks she is dead, and has not turned up in so good a place as she had reason to expect. She is a Mentonese, you know, and the Charing Cross Hotel is not exactly her notion of Paradise. I think this is mine. How dear of you to let me come!' Cordelia took in the chief beauties of Ivy Cottage in one admiring glance, and gave a long sniff at the sweet soft English air.

'I am glad to see you, my dear; I hope we shall make you happy. When did you cross?'

'Yesterday, in time for the Epsom week. Papa was full of dark engagements for to-day, so I hopped off early—*sans adieu.*'

'Did not your father see you off?'

'Oh, no. He will say it showed more tact than he thought me capable of to spare him the fuss of leave-taking.'

'We had better have some tea. Then you can write to announce your safe arrival.'

'It will be of no use to write. They are going into lodgings, and I do not know where,' said Cordelia, placidly, as they passed into the house.

Next day there was discussion on the subject of Cordelia at Wastel Warren. Mayne Wastel, the master of the house, said to his step-mother, the head of the family, 'Aunt Susan has caught a Tartar.'

'Oh, has she come!' said Mrs. Wastel.

'Have you seen her?' asked Lettice, sole daughter of that house, and the second Mrs. Wastel's only child.

'I looked in at Ivy Cottage this morning on my way from the Board, and found Aunt Susan quite off her balance, not sure if she should laugh, or cry, or be very angry. I advised the first, as soonest mended, and set her a good example when I heard that this young hussy had actually run away from her parent to come here, and arrived with only the clothes she stood up in—queer ones they are. It seems that running away is a vice that goes in the family. She turned up unexpectedly yesterday, and the old maids are all in a twitter about the want of notice, and there is a complication, it seems, about the spare-room carpet. Aunt Susan is furious with the father, who appears scarcely to be a joy to his friends, and has neglected this poor girl till her great wish has been to get away from him.'

'I can quite believe that. But any kind of running away is a serious matter. I do not wonder that Aunt Susan is alarmed,' said Mrs. Wastel.

'Then she has never stayed in a private house before, certainly not in one like Aunt Susan's. Fancy her making little casual remarks when Aunt Susan read the Bible to the maids, and saying she thought the wise virgins a selfish lot—much as if she had never heard of them before. Then, instead of coming down to breakfast this morning, she sent for coffee upstairs.'

'What bad manners! I am afraid she is not at all nice,' said Lettice.

'I do not say that. In spite of the con-
sternation produced by a call for coffee in that
tea-drinking household, and the " putting out "
of the old maids, I saw that this young woman
had walked straight into Aunt Susan's heart.
Lettice will be nowhere. She is like the hen
with the ducklings—proud, but puzzled. I was
laughing at her when this Cordelia came in.'

'What is she like?' asked Lettice with
curiosity, and her mother with fear.

'A very fine young woman, tall and well
set up, with a handsome face and a child's
expression, good eyes and chin—I do not know
about her nose—curly dark hair all in a fuzz.'

'What will Aunt Susan say to a fuzz?'
said Lettice, who had a brown and shining
tête d'oiseau.

'Perhaps it may be mitigated, but only
shaving her head will work quite a cure. The
funny thing is that she is like Aunt Susan
herself.'

'She does not seem to be like her mother,'

said Mrs. Wastel, with the yearning sigh that always came with her mention of Rosina. Her stepson noticed the sigh, and wondered at the store of affection that had been lavished on this unsatisfactory Rosina.

'She is like Aunt Susan; she has the same bright eyes and understanding look, and holds her head up in the same way.'

'Is she fast and slangy?' asked Lettice, anxiously.

'Well, perhaps—not exactly. You will say so; but I should not call her slangy myself, though she talks all the slangs I ever heard of. Aunt Susan does not understand half she says; but she has a nice way, a little friendly manner, like a nice child.'

'We must have her here—don't you think so, mother?—and try to do her good,' said Lettice.

'Yes, it will help Aunt Susan, perhaps; I do not think Mayne will object, as he seems to be following the aunt's lead. I am bound to do something for this girl—she is my cousin, and my dearest friend's child.'

Mrs. Wastel made an early call on Miss Hooper, in her full district equipment of grey shawl, bundle and tin pail. Aunt Susan was in her garden, making her slow progress among her flower beds; she was flourishing her stick about and poking at any small weed that had got its unauthorised head above ground during the night, for she leant on a strong and willing arm; she was admiring the flowers, and Cordelia was admiring her. As even the back view of a pair of lovers, though walking on opposite sides of the path, will subtly but certainly proclaim their lovership, so did the aspect of Aunt Susan and her great-niece, even from the garden gate, advise Mrs. Wastel that they were knit together already in a close bond of affection.

'Here is the milkwoman,' said Cordelia.

After a little mutual 'taking stock' as the three gossiped together, Mrs. Wastel, to gain a little conversation, and to see if the new-

comer had any airs, asked Cordelia to carry
the tin pail as far as the almshouses. She was
perfectly ready both to carry the pail and to
conduct the conversation.

'I never heard of you till I came here; I
did not know mamma had any cousins. I only
knew of Aunt Susan.'

'Yet I loved your mother very much, and
was her closest friend. I knew your father a
little too; perhaps he does not like to speak
much of your mother.'

'Very likely not, if he were nasty to her.'

'I did not mean that; I thought he might
still feel the sorrow of her early death.'

'Not he! Sometimes he slangs me for being
like her, or not like her, as it may happen.
Fancy the Colonel with a secret grief!'

'Was he willing for you to come here?'

'We had a tremendous shindy about it; but
I think he did not mind getting rid of me for a
time, and, as I was death on it, it had to be.'

'My dear!'

' There, I have said something again ! I am awfully sorry, for Aunt Susan does not like it ; and she is such a scrumptious old dear, I do not seem to care about riling her,' said Cordelia, looking full of compunction.

' The slang of the rising generation is always a trial to the one in possession ; and you must remember that, as Aunt Susan is two generations older than you are, it is doubly distressing to her. I wonder what were the forbidden expres- sions of her day ; there must have been plenty, for they seem to be a natural outcome of youth. The difference is that young people used to be obliged to restrain themselves, and now they have greater liberty of speech. We cannot imagine slang under the " nips and bobs " of poor Lady Jane's time, can we ? '

' I do not know. I have always talked as I liked, except at school, in French.'

' I suppose you have left school now for good, as school-girls say ? '

' I do not mean to go again, unless it is to

Brussels. I have been to so many schools, day schools chiefly, in France and England—cheap ones. I have learnt exactly nothing, except at the convent in Brussels—the *sœurs* there were first-rate, and one of them was Good.' Cordelia could always pronounce a capital.

'More than one, I hope. That was the place from which you were removed because Mr. Horley objected to a Romanist education for you?'

'Yes. How droll that you should know about me, when I knew nothing of you—don't I wish I had! That old boy did not know that the convent suited me down to the ground, and that I never learnt any religion at all.'

'I hope you learnt some of the right sort?'

'Do you care about it, really? How odd! So does Aunt Susie. No, I learnt none. I am as ignorant as a hobgoblin, and as bad as I know how to be ; and not on purpose, I am afraid it is nature. My work will be cut out when I set about being good, and it is time I began. Is your daughter good—the real sort?'

'Indeed, I trust so. Yes, Lettice is a very good girl.'

'Perhaps she can teach me; so few people seem to know. Aunt Susie is good, but I could not learn of her. I saw some one yesterday who looked as if he knew, and was like Sœur Lucie. It was the parson, the tall one; he was talking to a man in the lane, and I was sitting in the tree that leans over from Aunt Susan's garden.'

'The vicar, Mr. Odiarne. He is one of the best men I know.'

'I was sure of it! They do not have just that look unless they are of the best sort.'

'The oddest girl I ever saw; and I like her,' was Mrs. Wastel's report to her daughter and stepson; and she said very little more.

Lettice Wastel was more direct when she interviewed her cousin; she had fewer feelings on the subject, clearer views, and a more distinct object; youth has also fewer scruples, less experience of a daunting kind, and so fewer fears. Lettice meant to civilise, cultivate, and convert. 'How shall you employ yourself here?' she asked of Cordelia, a little later.

'The strawberries will not last for ever, I suppose,' said Cordelia, inspecting her red thumbs; 'but there are good things coming on —currants and raspberries, plums and pears, beside the peaches. The worst of plums and peaches is that you can gather faster than you can eat them; now strawberries take longer to gather than to eat, so you can always be going on.'

'You greedy thing! Aunt Susan's garden brings every one to that; Mayne calls every day in fig time. But are you not going to do something serious?—there is so much time here, and you are to make a good long visit, Aunt Susan says. I am so glad, for we shall have time to be really friends.'

'I am not very chummy with girls; they are always after something, and cannot let you rub along in peace. They do not often want

to be friends with me ; but if you do, I'll be on.
I dare say we shall scratch on somehow.'

Lettice, having come down from the Warren
carrying the precious boon of her friendship in
her hand to offer to this forlorn one, was hardly
gratified ; but she was perfectly patient, used to
small discouragements, and trained to hide her
passing feelings of annoyance. 'We will try.
I am rather jealous of you to begin with ; I
used to be Aunt Susan's first favourite, and you
have cut me out in a fortnight.'

'She thinks some pumpkins of you. She is
very good to me ; but I do not know—I do not
quite suit her, I am afraid ; she is always looking
at me through her spectacles as if I were the
queerest lot. Am I so awfully rum, do you
think ? '

Lettice laughed heartily, 'Yes, rather. You
have not been brought up like our Southshire
girls, and Aunt Susan does not see more than
one kind.'

'My kind is not quite right for her; perhaps

because I have been kept down, not brought up,' said Cordelia, deplorably.

'We might read something together,' suggested Lettice, seizing her opportunity.

'I do not like reading; there are so few nice books. I cannot get on with stories, for thinking what fools the people all are, and what a fuss they make about nothing. I suppose no one reads the other sort of books, except the fogies who really like what is stupid.'

'Oh, yes. Books that are not stories are the nicest, and you would like them best. It would be interesting for us to read the same . books and talk about them.'

'What kind of books?'

'I have been reading Grote's "History of Greece," and Mahaffy's books with it, and Worsley's "Iliad and Odyssey." We have "Gervinus" in the library-box; if you like we might read some Shakespeare.'

'We read Shakespeare at one of my schools. I do not think Mrs. Wastel would like you to read his book ; he uses so many bad words—downright swearing.'

'Perhaps you like something more modern, " Mrs. Somerville's Life," or " The Voyage of the Challenger "?'

'See here, Lettice ; this won't do at all, I shall never rise to this, I know.   You will have to drop me.'

'I cannot drop you, even if I wished, because you are my cousin.   There are plenty of nice things we can do together besides reading.'

'Why should I do anything? it is very nice to loaf round here, and talk to anyone that comes.'

'But do you not wish to be useful to people, to make your life of value to others?'

'Not in the least.   Do you?'

'I try,' said Lettice, modestly.   'Of course I know the world will go round without me, but I try to be of all the use in it I can.'

'That must make you a great nuisance to people, or it would if you were old and—not nice.   What do you do?'

'I manage the Uplands Sunday School, and go very often to the day school; I help the mistress and the pupil-teacher with their work. Then I have the penny bank and clothing club for the Uplands district; and I read with the younger servants, and go to the night-school sometimes, if Mayne goes. We have to help with things in Maybury, and as some of the property is in other parishes, there is always something on hand that we are expected to do. I have only been a year and a half without a governess, and my mother makes it my duty to read French and German—though I care for neither—and music is a duty, too, you know, in my position.'

'Good gracious! Do you do all this because it is right, and part of being good; or because you like it?'

'It is not very easy to say, though of course I ask myself the reasons and motives of my work sometimes. It is part of my life; I have grown into it, and. could hardly do otherwise. Some things I like very much, and others not at all; I hope I go through with the disagreeable part because it is right.'

'I suppose it is very horrid to be good at all?'

'Oh no! There is no other peace and satisfaction. Indeed, indeed, you must believe us when we say that. It is so hard to make people believe it, people who never think of doubting anything else we say. You may be sure of it, Cordie!' said Lettice, eagerly, thinking she saw an opening, and rising at once to the difficulties of her task.

'But if it is not horrid, and you only do it to feel jolly and set up with yourself, I do not see any goodness in it. You only do what you like, the same as the others,' Cordelia replied, with an air of deep disappointment. Before Lettice could marshal her arguments to meet her, she changed front, began to whistle the last air she had heard over the garden wall, and could not be brought to listen to any more moralising.

CHAPTER VII.

VARIED OUTLOOKS.

Health is the first good lent to men;
A gentle disposition then:
Next, to be rich by no by-ways;
Lastly, with friends t' enjoy our days.

R. Herrick.

CORDELIA was quickly at home with her new friends, so far as outward things went. She pervaded the garden at Ivy Cottage, and gossiped with the gardener and the maids. She took long solitary walks at all hours, which made Aunt Susan rather uneasy, until she recognised that something of the kind was necessary to work off her great-niece's spare energy. She sat a good deal in a tree that hung over the garden wall towards the road, and studied human nature from that novel outlook; but her chief playground, as well as school, was at the Warren, where Mrs. Wastel allowed her to come and go as she pleased, making her as one of the family.

The long shining summer days favoured this kind of life, and the girl learnt much. Those around her hardly guessed how much she had to learn, or how strange the even tenor of this English country life was, to one who knew nothing but watering-places, health resorts, and the people whose pleasure was their business. For reasons, Colonel Ashby never took this daughter with him on autumn visits to the sporting country houses where he was still received; and for reasons, different ones, Mrs. Lichfield never accepted for her sister sundry invitations to the very decorous and strait-laced houses of her husband's kindred; thus Cordelia regarded society from the hotel and lodging-house point of view, and had no key to the ways of such people as the Wastels. Aunt Susie was like an old lady in a book— only nicer, she thought; but for the Warren she had no standard.

The Wastels appeared to be rich—they had a large house in a small park, a butler, and many maids; two or three carriages, and horses to match, a liberal housekeeping, and no grumbling on money matters—and yet simple dress, that Mrs. Lichfield would have thought unwearable, old-fashioned furniture, plain food, no kind of display or extravagance, and a perfect indifference to comparison with their neighbours, or the opinion of outsiders; these things seemed contradictory. Then they were all so busy—they rose early, and worked hard at what they had in hand. Mrs. Wastel was often quite tired with her round of poor people and general benevolence, housekeeping, and letter-writing. Lettice chose her own occupations; yet she practised diligently, read German, and was busy with the works of which she had told Cordelia; she never dreamt of novels, tennis, riding, or visiting, till the afternoon, and then only in due subservience to things more important.

Mr. Wastel was still more perplexing. Many people who think it wrong for women and elderly persons to live for their own pleasure and amusement, make exception in the case of young men, grant them a liberty denied to their daughters, and, provided they have money enough to live on without their personal earnings, think it consistent with the right order of things that they should exist, not always beautifully, for their own delight. This slackness is a social mistake, for it takes much good breeding, as well as much money, to idle gracefully, while it is not at all difficult to work like a gentleman; a point which young men with more gold than gentle blood would do well to consider. Mr. Wastel's case was different, for he came of a family that had lived in honour as squires on the same property for five or six generations, and had usually followed some profession in their youth. For all Cordelia could see, there was no reason why he should not spend his time as her father and his friends did ; she knew they would think him a muff for not doing so, and she was a little inclined to be of their opinion at first.

But it was not for nothing that this girl came of the nearly extinct Hoopers, and of common ancestors with Aunt Susan. Her native wit supplied her lack of experience, and people even more young and foolish than herself could not have taken Mayne Wastel's pleasant brown face for that of a muff or any other description of fool, though his expression was more thoughtful than quick, and his neat, well-developed figure showed more energy than his face. He kept his body in good training, in working order as well as in subjection ; but his powers of mind being deep rather than agile, and at his age of seven-and-twenty not yet having come to their full power, he gave to the casual observer some impression of sternness. This impression was aided by his circumstances. At an age when many men are enjoying the pride of their youth, with all responsibility of life still on the shoulders of their elders, Mayne Wastel had relinquished one profession and devoted himself to another—one requiring many small sacrifices, and affording few opportunities for great ones, with no place for display or distinction, he had altogether come into his kingdom, and begun to live as he meant to die. Had he told his own history, which he was most unlikely to do, unless in time to come he should need to explain himself to the woman he loved—had he told his story, he would have said that there was only one event in it, certainly only one crisis, that had cost him doubt, pain, and sharp self-sacrifice, and that was clearly marked in his memory as the time when he held his life in his hand to turn it this way or that.

From the boy's birth Major Wastel intended his only son to go into the army, and brought him up accordingly. His own spear had been beaten into a pruning-hook in middle life, after a fair share of adventure and a moderate one of active service; his life having thus been interesting in its opening and satisfying in its close, he looked for the same for his son. Mayne's own tastes and powers led him to choose the scientific service; he passed out of Woolwich with honours, found the Engineers much to his liking, and spent in his corps several hardworking, hopeful, and very happy years. In an evil day for his son's career, Major Wastel fell ill of a lingering illness, which gradually sharpened his temper to an almost insupportable degree, and to a great extent weakened his judgment. He fancied that his property was going to rack and ruin when he could do nothing himself for its management; he grew suspicious of every one about him, and only placed confidence in his son, who was at a distance.

Mayne came home on leave when he could do so, and found things at Wastel Warren in a wretched state, to which his experience gave no parallel. His father was so ill that he must not be contradicted, and so well that nothing done in the house or on the estate escaped him; Mrs. Wastel was hollow-cheeked and worn, strained in body and mind almost to the breaking point; Lettice had been sent to school, and was dismally unhappy there; the bailiff had given warning; the agent was very nearly doing the same; and the doctor was only kept about his patient because he knew, what no one else but Mrs. Wastel would believe, that all this ill temper was only a 'symptom.'

For remedy, nothing would serve Major Wastel but that Mayne should give up the army and come home 'to look after things.'

'You must come after my death; come a little earlier; it will be my best comfort, and it will keep things together—if they go on like this much longer there will be nothing left for any of you.'

Mayne had by this time learnt that his

father's death could not be long delayed, and
had looked forward accordingly to duties and
necessities that must come. He had no thought
of giving up his beloved profession so soon as
he could live without it; the Warren estate
was not so large as to make it imperative for the
owner to live on it; and though Mayne loved
his home and the paternal acres as an Englishman should, he had not the same exclusive
devotion to them that his father had grown
into, and did not see 'that keeping things together' was his sole purpose in life. But it is
hard to resist a dying man, and that man an
honoured father, with whom his son had never
had a wrangle, much less a quarrel, in his
life.

Mrs. Wastel fought a good battle for her
stepson, and lost it.

'I have done all I can, Mayne,' she said,
with tears—'I have done all I can for you. If
you refuse, I will never blame you; but ask
Philip Odiarne, he is the only man who can

judge between you and your father; ask him, and abide by what he says.'

Mayne did consult his cousin, who had then but newly come to Maybury as Vicar, though in visits to his uncle's house he had learnt to know him and Mayne and their affairs. Mr. Odiarne, when he had heard all that was in Mayne's mind, appealed to Major Wastel, who gave in at the time, but with such evident misery that Mayne was overcome by his own victory and gave in on his side. Mr. Odiarne could not say to him 'do this or that'; but when, desiring only to do right, Mayne decided on his self-sacrifice, he gave him such consolation, encouragement, and sympathy, as made them friends for life, instead of, as hitherto, merely friendly cousins—and thus he gained something to set against his heavy loss.

After a few trying months Major Wastel died, and his son found that when the portions of his sister and his stepmother were taken from the estate he would be too poor a man to be justified in being an idle one. This deficiency was not from any failure of management or realisation of his father's fears, but from an unexpected depreciation of certain investments on which Major Wastel had relied to supply the charges on his estate. It was a hard case for Mayne that he should have given up his profession just when he most wanted it; but he never appeared sorry for himself. He applied for such appointments as his short service gave him chances for; but appointments are the slowest things in the world to come when they are wanted, and he turned his mind to some plans of his friends for semi-scientific travel, which were congenial and interesting, if not likely to be immediately profitable.

Mrs. Wastel proposed to live at Cheltenham, and leave the Warren to its heir; but one day when she was consulting him about a house there, he said: 'Why do you want to live at that hateful place?'

'It will suit us, I think, and not be more

hateful than another,' said Mrs. Wastel, surprised.

'What do you advise me to do with the
Warren?'

'If you travel for any length of time you
had better let the house. We will make your
home in England for as long and as often as
you like; that will be our holiday-time to look
forward to.'

'A pretty look-out! You and Lettice at
Villa No. 5,000, hating your lives; and I at
every grubby hotel and cut-throat public-house
between here and 'Frisco; with some fat grocer
from Maybury getting fatter at the Warren
while we break our three hearts for it!'

'Dear Mayne! I know; but we must make
the best of it.'

'Don't see the necessity. Look here, dear
lady '—and Mayne turned his back, and looked
very shy—' you are all the mother I have got,
and I don't want a better; and I am all the son
you have got, and you can't get a better; and

Lettice belongs to us both. Why can't you stay here and be comfortable? If you will, I will.'

'If it were right for you, my son?' said Mrs. Wastel, scrupulous but vanquished. Widowhood was sore enough to her, and she was young enough for a great shrinking from that villa life, with its narrow scope, its heavy society-tax, and, above all, its manufactured artificial duties, which every one seemed to think so very suitable for her, even waxing eloquent about the perfect lady's house, with its bright and cheerful drawing-room that she could fit up in the newest fashion after her own taste. Mrs. Wastel glanced round the large, rather shabby drawing-room at the Warren, with its miscellaneous pictures, furniture that was a fortuitous concourse of goods, and colouring that was an harmonious accident, and she loathed that bright cheerful room in prospect. She longed, too, that the flower-time of Lettice's life should be spent in her father's house and among his people, in the simple, healthful, dutiful mode of life that had grown up about his home, and in the wholesome companionship of such a man as her brother. For herself it was sweet now, in her sorrow, to feel a warm return for the strong love she bore her stepson.

'It will be right if you and I agree; but we can ask Odiarne,' said Mayne, with manifest pleasure. 'I cannot live here without your help, but with it we shall do well. I shall take the two Upland farms into my own hands, and turn into a constitutional Briton.'

'And what of the Rocky Mountains? You are giving up the plan that most interested you.'

'The Rocky Mountains will keep; nothing better. I do not seem to care about travelling if there is no Warren to come home to; it would lose its zest—like swimming, after your clothes have been stolen.'

'You will wish to marry some day, perhaps very soon.'

'Girls ought not to marry till they are twenty-one; you never know what they may turn out till they are at least as old as that. I must be ten years older than my wife, or I shall not have her in hand; that gives you and me just seven years to rub on together—we shall have time to marry Lettice, and look out for a good villa.' Mayne looked brighter than he had done since he gave up his commission.

This was four years before Cordelia Ashby came on to the scene. Mayne was now eight-and-twenty, and Lettice nineteen. Lettice had had two offers of marriage, but Mayne had not made even one. The home, as re-constituted had prospered well, and, whatever might be the end, they had four happy peaceful years to the good.

One hot June day Cordelia spent some hours at the Warren, following Mrs. Wastel or Lettice about the house and garden, taking a nap during the latter's after-luncheon hour of steady reading, but making Lettice give her a short sketch both of her subject at large and that day's portion of it, declining to help in some useful needlework, but condescending to lie in a hammock and watch its progress when Lettice sat down under the beech-trees that made the Warren summer parlour. It was Mayne's hammock; Lettice never used it, saying that bed once in twenty-four hours was enough for her. Cordelia made no defence, but asked for another cushion, and, with lazy body and active mind, lay looking up to the diaper of golden-green leaves upon the sky, and seeking for the secret of life at the Warren.

Before she could hit on the clue, the clang of the distant gate into the avenue was faintly heard through the afternoon stillness, then horse-hoofs, and the sharper clip of the gate near the house. 'It is Judith Carling,' said Lettice; 'she must have come to talk to my mother. She is always bringing her some sentimental difficulty or some religious straw to split. Mamma encourages her, when if she gave her a good slap and told her to mind her sick mother it would do her some good. Mamma enjoys nothing so much as a religious difficulty.'

'I thought religious people did not have difficulties, but went on all serene, you know.'

'I cannot see why they should,' said Lettice, reasoning from experience, 'but many of them have. It is because it is not necessary to be sensible to be religious I suppose. Judith's conscience is a constant plague; it worries her, or she worries it, till she is miserable, and then she rides six miles in a roasting afternoon to talk to my mother, who is sweetly sympathising. That comforts her till the next time she can have the horses, when she goes to some one equally good six miles off on the other side, who tells her something exactly different. If she would try to make the poor people at Longhurst send their children to school, her difficulties would be of another sort.'

From the drawing-room window came to

them a plump young woman in a riding-habit; she was about seven-and-twenty, with flat, colourless hair, a pale complexion, fine grey eyes, and rather a sad expression.

'Ah, Judith! have you been conferring with my mother? Come here and cheer up a little. This is my cousin, Cordelia Ashby.'

Miss Carling bowed absently towards the wrong end of the hammock, where Cordelia had placed her rush hat over her toes. 'Some one is claiming Mrs. Wastel's attention; a broken leg, I believe,' she said, in an injured tone.

'It is Jacky's hospital ticket; I must send word about it. Get up, Cordie, and talk to Judith,' said Lettice, very briskly.

Cordelia obeyed, startling Judith by sending her hat flying from the point of her left foot.

'Are you trying to be good?' she asked politely; and as Miss Carling did not seem quite prepared with an answer, continued, 'Most of the people here are good, it seems; I have come to the right place. Mrs. Wastel teaches you, does she not?'

'I think she has a great deal of sympathy; she understands one's secret longings after a purer and loftier atmosphere. I often take counsel with her,' said Judith, loftily.

'She is very good, I know, and so is Lettice and her brother; but they have not that—that power, you know—the tremendous force and go towards goodness that makes a few people such dabs at it.'

A smaller soul than Judith Carling's might have suspected a gibe, but she hardly noticed the incongruity of matter and expression.

'There are different natures; some are content with a humble level of mere action, like Lettice, and some aspire and yearn—I do that—towards heights of ineffable calm where all this miserable commonplace does not intrude.' She pointed with her riding-whip over the delicate blue distance divided by May-bury spire, and over the nearer slope of green tree-tops that fell softly down the hill-side from the Warren.

Cordelia was interested. 'I know the best people feel that calm within them, and they seem to be on a far-away height; but how is one to get there?'

'One must aspire, keep above all these petty miseries,' said the lady, making room for the tea-table; and in a lower voice, as Lettice returned, she added, 'We must keep ourselves away, free; abstract ourselves in an ecstasy of devotion, seek to breathe the divine incense— not this gross common air,' and she glanced up at the blue June heaven.

Mrs. Wastel followed Lettice, bringing a basket of strawberries—she was always carrying something good, said Cordelia; and the four ladies found their different philosophies meet very comfortably in a common taste.

CHAPTER VIII.

SCENES AND PROVERBS.

To be there as a friend   .   .   .   .
 Seem'd then, seems still, excuse for pride ;
For something that abode endued
 With temple-like repose, an air
Of life's kind purposes pursued
 With order'd freedom sweet and fair.

Coventry Patmore.

WHEN Miss Carling had gone, Mayne Wastel joined the other three, not without suspicion of having watched her departure.

'Well, Cordelia, you look oppressed. What did Judith say?'

'She says she yearns,' answered Cordelia, thoughtfully.

'For any one in particular?'

'I wish she did, then she could be killed or cured,' said Lettice.

'Not if it is for me. I am not equal to

either course,' said Mayne. 'She used to be rather jolly when we were little boys together, but now I flee from before her; she has addled her brain with trying to be clever, not guessing what a rare comfort a stupid girl is in these days.'

'I do not like you to laugh at her; she is really in earnest,' said Mrs. Wastel.

'She is a perfect owl!' said Lettice.

'She makes earnest ridiculous,' said Mayne.

'I used to feel very much as she does once.'

'Mother! what a libel on yourself.'

'What cured you, my lady?' said Mayne. 'Tell us, for we might try it on this interesting patient; but I cannot think you were so sad a case. What is sovereign for undigested metaphysics?'

'What cured you, mother?' repeated Lettice.

'My dears, I think it was your father. All that exaggerated feeling and sentimentalism was more common, and also more respected, in my day than in this ; your follies and exaggerations run in the opposite extreme, if I may hint that you have any. When your father's clear good sense was brought to bear on my mind, folly and effervescence calmed down. It was a great thing for a girl to be under such an influence, and I gave myself up entirely to it. I do not always know now which of my thoughts and opinions are my own, and which come of your father's teaching.' Mrs. Wastel spoke with a smile and a sigh, and there was a tender little blush on her faded cheek as she moved away from the younger ones.

'My mother could never have been such a goose as Judith ; but she always thinks herself guilty of other people's failings,' said Lettice, still fierce.

' " There, but for the grace of God, stands John Bunyan." That is her sentiment in presence of the wicked—not that Judith is to be named with such. What do you think, Cordelia ? ' asked Mayne, catching sight of her face.

'That if I were Miss Carling I should not want to be cured, as you call it. Is there anything wrong in wishing to be different—very good—as she does?'

'She only wants to talk about herself,' said Lettice.

'Nay, she means well; but I wish she would use ordinary methods and not talk " promiscuous." It would be a fine thing for her to fall in love.'

'To cure her of trying to be good?' said Cordelia.

'Not exactly; but it would have a startling effect upon her. Were you ever in love, Miss Ashby?'

'Never. Were you?' asked Cordelia, calmly. Lettice was aghast at her boldness, and thought Mayne foolish, especially when he answered,

'I have thought myself so sometimes, but I have seen reason to think myself mistaken very soon indeed; it had not been the real thing, I am afraid.'

'I have seen people make boiled owls of themselves over Sophy, and I have known girls go idiotic over a man, a heap of them at once ; but I never saw the real thing.'

'Not when your sister married?' asked Lettice.

'Not she ! Duncan must have been rather gone, for he asked her twice to marry him, and actually spoke to the Colonel. Sophy was mad at that, for she could have kept him floating a long time. When the Colonel heard of it he sat up four hours with her telling her of Duncan's advantages, and made her see it at last.'

'You should not repeat those things !' exclaimed Lettice, in deep disgust.

'I should hardly call that the real thing. When I see a good typical pair of lovers, I will point them out to you, and we will enlarge our minds at their expense. Only when your time comes, Mistress Cordelia, I wish you a more merciful chronicler than you are to your sister, and I shall take care that you do not tell my story. Come and have some tennis; it is cooler now.'

Lettice and her brother were great tennis-players. Lettice's firm little figure was as well poised and as active as a bird's, and she played with great neatness and precision pleasant to behold. Mayne was also a gratifying spectacle, and played well. The ground about the Warren was so undulating that it was difficult to find a good space for more than one court. The lawn they used was rather small. As they went to it, Lettice said, 'I think a ground could be contrived here, below the fence, without much digging.'

'Hardly room. Let us step it. Stand here, Cordelia. Eleven, twelve—now mark the corner, Lettice!'

'If this little hollow were filled up, there would be room,' said Lettice, looking critically along the short fine grass.

'It must be cut further back into the slope,'

said Mayne. 'No, ma'am, it will take too much navvy work.'

' Will it? Perhaps in the autumn? '

'Too big a job, till autumn twelve months, at least. It is a pity, for it would be sheltered from the wind. Well, "Quand on n'a pas ce qu'on aime, il faut aimer ce qu'on a ! '" said Mayne.

' I thought that was one of the devil's proverbs,' said Cordelia, naming the old gentleman without useless periphrasis, 'encouraging us to be content with lower things, just as "Chassez le naturel, il revient au galop" teaches us to leave our faults alone. Sœur Lucie said so when we were choosing proverbs to play.'

'Philip Odiarne says people quote " One may as well be hung for a sheep as a lamb " in excuse for one more sin,' remarked Lettice.

'I must save my character somehow,' said Mayne. 'I suppose even Solomon's " He that is surety for a stranger shall smart for it " is to be taken as worldly wisdom, and not as an excuse for selfishness.'

' Mayne speaks feelingly,' said Lettice ; ' he recommended a stray German to lodgings in Maybury, and then had to pay his bill ; and he will do it again for the next forlorn one. Now, Cordie, serve your ball and don't moralise."

' I shall never play,' said Cordelia. ' It is not my style.'

' Never say die ! Why not ? Do you mean to give way to idleness and Aunt Susan's cakes ? '

' It is not idleness, but it is not my style to hop about and look sharp, with my wits at the end of my bat. It suits Lettice ; it is her style to do quick brisk things.'

' And what is your style, if one may ask ? '

' To be majestic and quiet, to sit still and have people round me ; quite the ponderous swell, you know.'

' A stately queen—I can see you now, in

purple and gold and peacock's feathers. Very
good when you are forty, but in the mean time
I advise tennis, for if you get too fat you will
spoil the effect,' replied Mayne, laughing. He
could well picture Cordelia as a stately beauty,
although, in spite of the lavish expenditure of
two hundred and eighty ill-gotten francs on her
wardrobe, there was still a good deal of the
ragamuffin in her appearance. She took the
racquet he handed her, and, with the ready
docility that made half her popularity, took a
rather successful lesson.

'Now, you do like it?' said Mayne, as she
paused, looking very bright and flushed with
success, though not with victory.

'Yes, I like playing with you, and feeling
that I can do it a little; but I should not care
to play much—it is not like walking or riding,
that give one time to think.'

'Is that it?' said Mayne, looking at her
quizzically, but with understanding.

He left them after a game with Lettice, and

Cordelia said to the latter, ' Why did you not stick to it? You would have got your new tennis-ground with a little coaxing or bullying, whichever may be the right way with your brother.'

'Very likely; but Mayne is doing several expensive things just now—some draining that will improve the North Upland Farm; and there is a very pet scheme for some better cottages.'

'But he would like it himself, better than dirty drains and cottages.'

'I could not use my influence to persuade him to do what is not right, or to neglect important duties for our own pleasure,' said Lettice, loftily.

'Do you think your influence is as tall as that?' said Cordelia, not the least impressed.

Lettice laughed, nothing offended. 'No; it is a long way short. Cart-ropes would not make him do anything really wrong; but he is so kind that I meant he might wish to please me at the expense of things important to his interest.'

' Is he good ? '

' Of course he is ; no one better.'

' But he laughs at your Sunday school and at Miss Carling, and he said strong things about that revival meeting.'

' Do you mean, is he religious ? Yes. We women talk and preach, but few of us are as good as Mayne. He never has the things he likes best, but he never grumbles ; and he does not laugh at good work, only at me for making too much fuss. Mayne has the right thing, deep down. He says nothing, but one is sure of him.'

' You all seem to be good here, even the young men.'

' And why not the young men ? One good man is worth three good women. I am not sure that they are more rare, but they don't pretend.'

' They do not always take to it like ducks

to a pond. Nor do I, worse luck! I do not
see my way at all yet,' Cordelia ended, with a
sigh.

'Oh, Cordie, if only I could help you! I
know Aunt Susan's ways are not always just
suited to girls ; and as for the clergy—men do
not always understand, and I dare say you are
shy of them. I shall be so very glad if I can
help you.'

'Thank you, but you can't at all; I do
think you are as good a girl as I know, but it
must be a——' Cordelia was beginning to
drop some of her flowers of speech as she learnt
which of them distressed her new friends, but
this time her only resource was to say, 'a very
dab hand at it.'

The girls parted, and Cordelia, full of
thought, went down the Maybury road towards
Ivy Cottage. It was a warm, cloudy evening ;
she took her hat off her tangled head and
swung it over her shoulder on her red parasol,
and never noticed that as she walked along the

frequented road many people turned to gaze at her—a party of young men returning from a cricket match, two or three more on bicycles, the Vicar going to dine at the Warren, Mr. Horley for his evening ride, a carriage full of people coming from the station, and a good many young couples bound for a country stroll. Most of them stared at Cordelia—the cricketers, I regret to say, cheered her; only the Vicar did not appear to see her, and the Vicar was the only person Cordelia noticed, as she recognised his thin face in a hansom cab. ' *Voilà mon affaire !* ' she thought, ' if I can but manage it.'

Aunt Susan was in the garden in her favourite position commanding the gate and the passers-by. She knew exactly who had passed during the last quarter of an hour, what their objects were, and who would meet Cordelia.

' Dearest Aunt Susie, how sweet to find you glad to see me ! I never remember my elders and betters glad to see me in all my life !

'I have been looking for you; it is nearly our tea-time. I fear you have not left Lettice time to dress for dinner.'

'Oh, Lettice will soon tumble into her clean frock!'

'And, my dear, have you come all the way down like this—without your gloves, and your hat off? You would meet Mr. Odiarne, and the Kilburne carriage ——'

'I am afraid I met all Maybury. I never thought you would mind. I am awfully cut about it since you do. Here is a note from Mrs. Wastel. I know what is in it, and I don't want to go.'

'Gently now! Julia never learnt to write a really ladylike hand; and what absurd paper! You are asked to the Warren to go to the *fête* at Sir John Somers', and to stay a few days. That will be nice for you.'

'I had rather stay with you, Aunt Susie. I have only been here a fortnight, and I feel more at home than ever I did in my life.'

'It is only for a few days ; an old woman is not enough for a child like you, and I wish you to be at the Warren ; it is good for you.'

'Do you wish me to be like Lettice? I think it will not be much use to try. She is not bad, but she is not my style. I should not make much out of trying to be like Mrs. Wastel either ; though I think, next to you, she is quite the too most awful duck I ever spotted.'

'You are the most awful quite a goose. If you and I are to be friends we must speak the same language ; and as you do not learn mine very quickly, I must learn yours. I hope you think it suits my cap and stick ? '

'How you laugh at me ! so does Mayne ; but when I say rummy things, without meaning it, Lettice looks unutterable, and I feel vile. Mayne would make the best model, and learn me manners best.'

'Certainly, if you were a young man ; but as you are not, it would be more modest to propose his sister as your model.'

Cordelia blushed furiously, and looked offended. 'I suppose you mean I am not to be so go-ahead ; " modest " is a cracker of a word to use ? '

'Words alter their force as years go on. I only intended a very light rebuke, my dear. To be as dutiful and unselfish as Mayne Wastel would be good for man or woman. Have you dresses suitable for this visit ? ' with a glance at her niece's costume, which bore traces of the hammock.

'Yes, auntie. That new dark-blue frock for morning; the black with red ribbons for evening ; and for the *fête*, I have a gown that Sophy got in Paris, white—it is all right, I think,' said Cordelia, confidently. She had spent her ten pounds cleverly, and had never been so well fitted out before. Miss Hooper had seen the dark-blue and the black gowns, works of a Mentone dressmaker, and took the white one on trust, as a younger woman would not have done.

CHAPTER IX.

FAIR PASSAGES.

O day most calm, most bright,
The fruit of this, the next world's bud.

G. Herbert.

THE great event of the Maybury neighbourhood during this summer was the coming of
age of Sir John Somers' eldest son, and most
of the country-houses near were filled with
visitors for the *fête*. At the Warren were
Captain Longley, once a brother officer of
Mayne Wastel's, with his young wife, a stout
handsome little woman, who admired herself
and her married position immensely; and Mr.
Conyngham Sedley, a London man, approach-
ing middle age, whose family had once resided
in the county, and who was everybody's old
friend. He represented himself as full of engagements in this early July, and as being only

torn with great difficulty from the friends to
whom he was necessary in town; but it was
well understood that he had looked forward
for months to this visit to Wastel Warren, and
would stay as long as he could stretch his
invitation. Mr. Odiarne was also to be of the
Warren party. Cordelia's handsome young
face and bright considering eyes made a nota-
ble addition to the circle. She did not talk
much, though she responded readily when ad-
dressed. Neither she nor Lettice were noisy,
or inclined to flirt or to become excited with
talking, and this for exactly opposite reasons.
Lettice was proud, well trained, and self-
respecting, as well as a very little self-conscious; she never forgot her manners. Cordelia
looked on herself as of no account; she was
absolutely unembarrassed and perfectly simple
in all her ways; treated every one, old and
young, male and female, with exactly the same
calmness; was deeply interested in other people,
and never dreamt that any one could be in-

terested in her, or care for what she said or
did.

Some of the neighbours dined at the Warren
on the Saturday. Mrs. Wastel remarked that
being a Saturday she could not have a large
or late party, puzzling Cordelia a good deal.
What difference could the day of the week
make? It was the latter's first experience of
English country society; she admired, but was
awed. Mrs. Wastel's handsome evening dress
showed off the old-fashioned type of her beauty,
which belonged to the bygone time when softness and grace were admired, and ' elegance '
was sought after; when a delicate complexion
was cherished, and a white and shapely forehead was a feature not to be concealed. Dress
made very little difference to Lettice. She
looked the same trim and neat little woman at
all times, and went about her social duties with
the same completeness and accuracy that she
brought to all her occupations, perhaps with
the same shade of complacency.

Mrs. Wastel was a very good musician, and played both piano and harp with great taste and delicacy.   Lettice's lesser powers had been carefully cultivated, and she sang well.   Mayne sang better, and had a fine voice ; but their chief musical allies were absent this evening ; and, as a relief from strictly family music, Mrs. Wastel asked Mrs Longley to sing.   She declined ; and Mayne, while she was still making her excuse, casually asked Cordelia if she did not sing ; he thought he had heard her.   ' Oh, yes, I will sing, if you like,' she answered obligingly, and without further invitation or prelude struck a single note on the piano, near which she stood.   She sang a rollicking little French song in praise of wine, in a fresh, strong, quite uncultivated voice.   Some of the gentlemen thought it and the singer charming ; but Mr. Conyngham Sedley lifted his eyebrows high in response to Mrs. Longley's glance. Lettice, whom the jovial measure brought from the other end of the room, expressed her relief

that it was French, and no worse. She knew
some of Cordelia's songs.

Sunday morning at the Warren was fresh
and shining. The very flower-beds looked
calm and orderly. The scent of the hay from
one field suggested placid waiting for Monday,
while the clean raked surface of another told
of work finished on Saturday. There was no
post-bag till midday, at which Mr. Sedley
meant to grumble, but forgot. Lettice was in
a white frock, but was so far out of harmony
with the scene as to wear a business face: the
Sunday school was on her mind; nothing, and
no one, must keep her from it. She was also
desirous that all the party should go to the
Uplands for service; a tiny church, served by
the Maybury clergy, and where she, Lettice,
was general director; and that they should not
stray away for possible town attractions at
Maybury. Mrs. Wastel answered for herself
and Mrs. Longley. Captain Longley asked
which walk was the coolest, and Mr. Sedley

declared that the whole Sunday duty of country ladies was to 'set a good example,' and he
would help Lettice in this, to him, novel func-
tion.   Then there was Cordelia.

'May I go with you, Lettice, and see a
Sunday school?' she asked.

'Oh, yes!   I should like to show you how
we manage.'

'Miss Ashby is not of the Sunday-school
pattern.   Will she be up to pranks?' asked
Conyngham Sedley of Mayne, as they stood on
the portico and watched Lettice set off with an
armful of books, accompanied by Cordelia, the
correctness of whose Sunday attire was marred
by the shabby red parasol with its bull-dog
handle.

Across the large park-like field that gave
its name to the Warren, and by a deep green
lane, they came to the Uplands Church—a
very venerable building indeed, on which
learned, and therefore wary, archæologists
spoke in the most guarded and uninstructive

terms. Painters, who are a freer folk, loved
the pure silver grey of the low thick walls,
and the steep and high-tiled roof, which was of
every colour that time all-softening, lichens
white and orange, and mosses brown and
green, can turn a roof that no living man
remembers to have been red. The hillocky
churchyard was enclosed by stout oaken posts
and rails, on which were perched about forty
of the Uplands children. At sight of ' Miss,'
and on this occasion of ' one with her,' they
scampered off to a small schoolhouse adjoining
the churchyard, and sorted themselves into
order before Lettice arrived and took the command, a small but efficient captain. Her two
lieutenants, the village schoolmistress and a
farmer's daughter, appeared a minute later,
and read in Lettice's eye that they were that
minute behind time. She read prayers, called
over names, distributed books, and presently
established Cordelia in a chair on one side of
a hollow square, with nine middle-sized boys

filling the other three sides. 'Now, boys, you must be very good with this lady, as she is kind enough to teach you. Jimmy! What are you thinking of? Give me those bulls'-eyes immediately!' Jimmy meekly handed over a small sticky screw of newspaper, which Lettice pocketed without a shudder. 'Hear them say their collects and hymns, and then give them a lesson on the Second Commandment,' she whispered to Cordelia, who began to wish she had taken Mayne Wastel's hint and declared for Maybury Church.

They were nice little boys, Cordelia thought, on a second glance, and it would be easy to make friends with them. They were very much alike, with flaxen hair, blue eyes, and pink cheeks; but one, who was pale, with brown hair and a sad look, reminded her of Fero, and made her heart long for the child. This boy had learnt the collect, and would by no means be disappointed of rehearsing it, in a high voice at a wonderful

speed, with his eyes stonily fixed on the
wall above Cordelia's head. Another boy followed, saying something else. He was rebuked
for this by the head boy, who, finding that
Cordelia was deaf to his insinuations—' It be
the wrong un ; it be last Sunday ; he ain't
learnt it '—at last found the place in a prayer-
book, and summarily convicted her of not
knowing which Sunday after Trinity it was.
' She dunno, she doan't,' was whispered round
the class, and Cordelia felt that she must do
something to revive her failing prestige. ' Do
you say hymns ? ' she asked. This produced
another book, and the boys repeated each some
verses with much decorum, and Cordelia felt
afloat again.

One of the hymns repeated went to a
popular tune, and Cordelia began to hum it
in brisk time, giving it an airy and dancing
tilt, which the tune bore better than the
words. The boys were delighted, and took it
up vigorously ; but they were hardly in swing

when a peremptory message came down the
room from Lettice. They must not sing now,
and would Miss Ashby keep her class quiet?
This was not so easy, but a glance at the boy
who was like Fero inspired her. She took her
parasol and twisted her handkerchief round it
to make a body for the bull-dog's head, the
boys looking on with breathless interest as she
cleverly twisted the corners to make his fore-
paws and his curly tail. Then announcing him
as the real dog Toby, she began a little play with
him that had often been little Fero's joy. The
boys, silent at first, began to snigger with
delight, then to laugh aloud, and very soon
there was an uproar that threatened to involve
the whole school. All at once, as the boys
were clustered about Cordelia's knee, an awe
fell upon them, their faces stiffened from their
grins, though their mouths remained open;
they sank back into their places and gazed,
wondering what might befall.

A grave voice behind Cordelia said, 'Are

the boys troublesome? Perhaps you are not used to them.' Looking round, she saw Mr. Odiarne, his tall head far above her, casting inquiring glances at the boys, at her, and at the dog Toby, who grinned unabashed at him from the parasol stick.

'I wanted to keep them quiet,' she murmured, feeling that things had somehow gone wrong.

'Give me your place for a few minutes. Sit here, if you will, on the bench.'

Cordelia gladly subsided, and after a question or two, till the boys had recovered the just balance of their behaviour, Mr. Odiarne began to give them a lesson. It was on the Good Shepherd. He spoke so clearly that Cordelia, really more untaught than the least of the boys, listened with deep interest, amazed also to find how much these children knew as they unfailingly answered the scientifically put questions. Then the Vicar went on to speak of the Shepherd's love and tender care, and Cordelia's eyes swam and the tears even dropped over, as her heart swelled and filled with the sense of consolation, and as the aching places in it were touched. The little boys listened gravely and with evident enjoyment, but they were not too much absorbed to see Cordelia's tears, nor to confide to each other as they filed out of the schoolroom that 'She were a rum 'un, she were; and she must reckon she were agoing to catch it. Gyals always cried when Muster Odiarne he give it 'em.'

It was unusual for the Vicar of Maybury to take the morning service at Uplands, the dignity of his office requiring him to be at the parish church; but to-day a stranger was preaching there, and he was free for a duty that he particularly liked. He took the whole service, and preached a simple direct kind of sermon from the lectern. Cordelia listened as she had never listened before; Mr. Odiarne seemed so near, and his words to come with the force of an individual address, more personal and closer than when he took part in the stately service in the great church at Maybury, or preached from the lofty pulpit to the crowded, intelligent, and eager congregation who liked to have an intellectual exercise as well as, or for their own choice much better than, a spiritual instruction.

'What a treat to have Philip here!' said Mrs. Wastel, as they all walked home together.

'I think I like him best when he brings down, or, I had better say, condenses his great powers to an old woman's sermon.'

'It was nice and short,' said Mrs. Longley.

'Odiarne is a very good hand—too good for the rustics; he should get a London church,' said Mr. Conyngham Sedley.

'I like him best at Maybury,' said Lettice; 'when he gives one really something to think of and work out—not a mere Sunday-school lesson, as to-day.'

'Which Miss Wastel of the Warren could have given as well?' whispered Mayne to her, with a glance at Cordelia, who was close by, that met with no response.

'Yes,' said Lettice, simply; 'so I like to learn something to add to my store.'

'What do you say, Miss Ashby?' asked Captain Longley, who admired her, and liked to draw her out, as he called it.

'I have no store, only an empty basket; while Lettice's is full and bursting. I think I can put a nut in mine to-day. I never listened to a sermon before.'

'You are honest. What a mind you must have to entertain yourself through all the sermons you have to sit through. I am afraid I often listen from pure vacancy.'

'I do not often go to church — Sophy seldom goes—and I do not like it much yet; some day I suppose I shall.'

Mrs. Longley heard this. She had her doubts about Cordelia: the girl was so evidently new to the sort of life the Wastels led; her style was so odd; she must have had a queer bringing up; there was a screw loose somewhere. Mrs. Longley was sure that her own screws were tight, and so found it agreeable to finger other people's, to make certain that there was not a little exciting slackness here and there. Mr. Odiarne overtook them here. Mrs. Longley was minded to say a word about Cordelia, but was deterred; she knew not why.

'Cordie, you got on pretty well with your class for a first attempt, though you must learn to keep the boys a little quieter,' said Lettice, kindly, when they were alone. The bull-dog expedient had been lost on Lettice, absorbed with her big girls.

'I will not try again. I must learn something myself—from Mr. Odiarne if I can. He spoke *so* to the children; those little scamps listened! And I was a pulp in no time.'

'Dear Cordie, we will all teach you, and you will be the best of pupils!' Lettice stood on tip-toe to kiss Cordelia's cheek, which was not at all bent towards her.

Before Mr. Odiarne left the Warren after luncheon, Lettice caught him. 'I am coming down the avenue with you, Philip; I want to ask you something—it is not an old woman this time, but a young one—Cordelia Ashby.'

'What of her? Do you wish to beg pardon for having set her down to teach in my Sunday school without leave?'

'No. I found, however, that I had made a mistake; she does not know how to keep order.'

'There are two or three more little things that she does not know. I thought you were a wiser superintendent than that, Lettice. Never mind. What do you want to say about her?'

'I want you to see to her a little, Cousin Philip; though she is so wild and has been so queerly brought up, her great wish is towards better things, and she wants teaching.'

'Does she want to be taught?'

' Yes, I meant that.'

' You may find her above your hands as a pupil.'

' I have offered to help her more than once, but she flies off; and though she loves dear Aunt Susan, and seems to think great things of my mother, she is not willing to be taught by them. She would listen to you, I know.'

' Knox looks after the young women ; she had better be under him.'

' I am afraid Cordie would laugh at him ; she calls him——'

' Never mind what! I am sure she has great powers of characterisation.'

' Yes,' said Lettice, laughing. ' But she has also really serious aspirations, and I want so very much to do her good. You will talk to her, Philip ; no one will be of so much use to her as you will.'

' I must take your word for it that she is in earnest. I have small faith in my powers of doing any good to a flippant young person who only wants to be amused, and will bestow some sticking nickname on me for my pains—not that it will do any harm to me, but I cannot have her ridicule serious things.'

' You know I would not risk that.'

' Well, I will think of it, for Aunt Susan's sake as well as for your asking.   I am going with you to the Silverwood *fête* to-morrow, and I will take another look at your cousin.'

CHAPTER X.

A GUIDE.

And there evermore was music, both of instrument and singing,
  Till the finches of the shrubberies grew restless in the dark;
But the cedars stood up motionless, each in a moonlight ringing,
  And the deer, half in the glimmer, strewed the hollows of
    the park.

E. Barrett Browning.

THE *fête* at Silverwood, to celebrate the coming
of age of Sir John Somers' heir, was a com-
prehensive entertainment, beginning, so far as
the gentry were concerned, with a dinner on a
scale that seemed to require the use of the word
'banquet;' going on to fireworks so soon as the
summer night would darken sufficiently to
allow of strange fires; and ending with a ball.
Earlier in the day the tenantry were enter-
tained, and before them the labourers and the
school-children. Sir John, who had married

late in life, and was the father of three daughters before his much-desired eldest son was born, was glorious on this day, and by far the happiest person present. Lady Somers looked a little anxious and tired as she stood, a fair conventional woman, who always struggled up to what was expected of her, between her husband and her son, and replied bravely to yet another batch of congratulations; but Sir John was quite fresh, though he had made four speeches that day and looked forward to two more. He beamed on all the world, fairly anticipated congratulations, listened to nothing that was said to him, and looked on the younger John as if that worthy had taken a city, instead of merely thriving on the fat of the land for twenty-one years.

Mrs. Wastel, in full sympathy with her neighbour's joy, said the prettiest possible things to her hosts and to the hero of the day.

'You poor Jock, shall you pull through?' was Lettice's salutation to the heir.

'I am bearing up; thanks. Keep the second waltz for me. Wish it was come! Lots to go through before then,' whispered Jock, hurriedly. He was a plain youth, with a square frowning brow, and a wide mouth that would look better when he had a little more moustache; but he was unexceptionable in everything but looks, and he was a general favourite. Mayne's greeting to him was a compound of nod and wink, that conveyed sympathy, encouragement, and a hope of meeting when better times should come.

Miss Ashby was presented in due form to the seniors—the young Somers' had met her before—and the Wastel party moved on. Miss Somers met them—a tall fair-haired girl, like her mother, but with more originality and force of character. 'You dear people! How glad I am to see some one to whom I need not be polite. Caro and I have been at it for seven hours already; this is my third clean frock and second box of gloves; and all the time we feel such inferior creatures, such mere women;

while Tim and Toby, who are nearly as good fellows as Jock on other days, are made to feel their junior position acutely. Not one of us dare to go near Jock for fear of catching his eye, or if once he laughs it is all over with him.'

In spite of her complaints Charlotte Somers looked well and spoke at her best. She was excited to just the right pitch of animation by the knowledge, or rather the feeling, that there was some one standing near in whose eyes she could do no wrong, and in whose ears the simplest word she said was perfection.

Tim and Toby, hereafter to be known to fame as Theodore and Alexander Somers, now came up. They were taller, better-looking, and more assured young men than their elder brother, and, though the estate was strictly entailed, they were lighter of heart on this particular evening.

'Poor Jock,' said Tim, 'all his dances are cut out for him. He may dance once with

Lettice, but he won't get a turn with Miss Ashby because she is a stranger. I shall cut Lettice because she snubbed me about the volleys the other day, and dance with Miss Ashby as often as she will let me.'

'Don't you talk!' said Toby; 'Mayne, he has to do Miss Prigeon and Mrs. Waddell before he may look out for himself, and as I am but a youth I am let off with Miss Martindale.'

> 'And a very nice girl you'll find her ;
> She'll pass very well for forty-three
> In the dusk with the light behind her,'

chanted Cordelia, gaily, in not too low a voice.

Miss Somers looked round nervously ; Toby was delighted. Mr. Odiarne, who had heard the words but not their application, put on a comical face, and looked at Lettice.

'Come, Cordelia, and look at Jock's teapottings, and don't bear so hard; any of us may be forty-three some day,' said Mayne, taking the rash young creature to the other end

of the long drawing-room.   Lettice gazed after
them anxiously.   Mrs. Longley made an expres-
sive gesture as she said, ' Did you see her before
she got into the carriage?   I did not, or I
would have warned you.   Where can she have
laid hands on such a thing? '

The ' thing ' in question was Cordelia's
gown ; it was only in part responsible for
Lettice's look, but a hard little woman like
Mrs Longley could not be permitted to tread
on tender places.   The gown was certainly a
grievance, even to people far less sensitive in the
matter of clothes than Mrs. Longley.   It was
of white cashmere, slashed with red satin and
trimmed with gold braid—harmless materials
enough, but the costume was made in Paris for
Mrs. Lichfield to wear at a fancy ball ; the whole
style of it was so fast—it was so audaciously
kilted up in one place and let down in another, it
was so short in front and so long behind, that
Cordelia's tall figure and handsome vivacious face
were made altogether too conspicuous.   Besides,

the white was dimmed, the satin frayed, the gold
tarnished, so that the garment was more like
an old theatrical property than the companion
of the fresh, correct, and rather prim and stiffly
worn dresses of the English country girls.
Cordelia had not thought twice on the matter;
she had a fine gown—not so fresh as she could
have wished, but undoubtedly fine, and good
enough for her, Cordelia, a person of no
account. She heartily admired Lettice in soft
cloudy white, like a cotton-grass tuft, though
wishing some broad touches of decided colour
were added. 'Lettice has so much character;
she is not that vaporous kind of person really,
and her dress should be distinct too.' She also
saw that Mrs. Longley, in an arrangement of
shining blue and green, with dots of coral
pink, very tight, well padded and important,
looked like a pigeon—a resemblance that she
pointed out to Mayne; but she never thought
of her own dress, nor of the effect she might
produce.

For the great dinner in the tent Tim Somers provided Miss Ashby with a partner in their London lawyer's son—a young man on whom he could thoroughly depend—and bade him place her on his, Tim's, right hand. Captain Longley was opposite to them, with a very lively young married lady; and the fun at that table, somewhat removed from the elders and betters in the chief seats, was fast and furious. Mayne Wastel, with Judith Carling, was near enough to see much and hear a little, but too far off to join. Judith was very metaphysical and abstruse; his head was bent towards her, but his gaze went beyond, to the spot where his young guest was making a fool of herself in such a very bewitching manner that he wished on all accounts he had been nearer. He hoped that Lettice was out of earshot.

'We must consider Thought quite apart from the thing thought of—Thought as Thought in the abstract. If we are not able to throw ourselves outside of ourselves, and watch the operations of our own minds ——' Judith was saying, when her neighbour's earnest look attracted Cordelia's glance. Not content with replying in kind to his little nod of recognition, it entered into her head to testify her regard by throwing at him a large pink sugared almond from the cracker she had just pulled with Tim. Just at the moment when there arose above the din the trembling accents of poor Jock, once more returning thanks for the flattering terms in which, &c., &c.—flop! went Cordelia's missile right into Miss Carling's glass of champagne, sending the cheering liquor into her eyes, and breaking the glass with a clash. Judith squeaked aloud; some one else thought it must be a bullet as the likeliest thing to come skimming down the table at that juncture, and screeched in concert. Cordelia's neighbours betrayed her by giggles and laughs that amounted to an interruption of the speech. Jock broke down, and about half the guests, in their indignation or amusement, forgot the applause that would have covered everything.

During the fireworks Cordelia was missing;
but when the dancing began she was found to
be well provided with partners among a number
of young men, who, being admitted to Silverwood on rare and great occasions only, were a
little oppressed with the burden of an honour
unto which they were not born. They intro-
duced themselves or each other to Miss Ashby,
and made a little subsidiary queen of her.
Lettice, popular as well as pretty, was in great
request as a partner among her own set; but
though much occupied, she had time to feel
greatly hurt and annoyed when she came across
Cordelia, with her loose hair and her undesirable
gown, dancing with young Taylor from the
Maybury bank, or Horace, known as 'Horrid'
Greeson, the agent's son—youths who did not
dream of the honour of dancing with the county
princesses, and for whom a sufficient number of
each other's sisters and cousins had been duly
provided.

Cordelia, though a novice in society, and

disposed to make her own laws, yet observed that when Mayne asked her to dance her followers fell back respectfully. One with whom she was about to stand up, murmured, like Mr. Toots, that 'it was of no consequence,' and effaced himself. Cordelia thought this was only due to the natural superiority of everything belonging to the Warren, and, pleased at Mayne's cousinly treatment of her, went off chattering gaily. After their dance he took her to Mrs. Wastel, who had not seen her since dinner. After sitting near her a little while in the seats of honour, Cordelia remarked that her next partner would never venture to fetch her from there, and walked down the ballroom to meet him under all the eyeglasses of the august matrons.

'Who is that girl?' asked Lady Isabel Kingdon of Mayne, as Cordelia passed them.

'She is my sister's cousin—my half-sister's, that is—Miss Ashby. She is staying with us. She is a child in most things, but she is fresh caught from no bringing up at all. She is a very jolly little thing, but she looks odd to-night. That is a queer get-up; Lettice ought to have seen about it.'

'Quite dreadful kind of girl, I should say!' said Lady Isabel, calmly.

'Is she not the daughter of a man they call Greyleg Ashby; and did he not run away with her mother, uncommon pretty girl?' asked old Sir William Torwell, who stood by.

'Yes; do you know him?' said Mayne.

'Did once. Too shady a lot for me now. By Jove! young Wastel, that girl will want looking after! Comes of a bad stock, you know. Don't go and marry her without a warrant. Those things run in families; bolting is in the blood, and other things—gambling, for one.'

'Cannot they be trained out, if you begin early?' asked Mr. Odiarne, as Mayne and his partner moved away.

'Don't know much about girls—never had one,' replied Sir William. 'Don't suppose

they are any easier to train than horses. Horse
with a bad temper is worth the trouble if he is
all right otherwise. Girl has got good points,
but she will want a good deal of lunging to
bring her into form.'

'I think I will try,' said the Vicar to himself.

Later in the evening, when Mrs. Wastel
asked for Cordelia, Mr. Odiarne volunteered to
look for her. He heard of her as having gone
towards a pavilion in the grounds, which had
been lighted and decorated as a place for
lighter refreshments. Sounds of laughter and
song came far down the shrubbery-walk that
led to the spot. As he drew nearer, the song
became plain as an Italian street song, almost
too festive a strain, that the singer, our Cordelia, had picked up from some Neapolitan
street musicians on the Riviera. For the more
effective rendering of this choice bit, she was
standing on the end of a little balustrade which
enclosed the steps leading up to the pavilion,

and she was accompanying herself on a child's tambourine which had been left there, and had, indeed, suggested the performance. No other ladies were then at the pavilion, nor were Tim or Toby visible; Cordelia's applauding audience consisted of four or five of the odd young men aforesaid, some of whom were smoking, of several servants and waiters, and of two old gentlemen who had been all the evening within easy distance of the refreshments.

'Tra-la-la' went the song, 'ting-a-ting-ting' the tambourine, when Mr. Odiarne's tall straight figure and quiet uplifted face came within the circle of light from the pavilion lamps. He did not look at all severe, for he was smiling a little at a thought that had come to him as he passed through the cool dusk garden; nor did he take in the details of the scene before him very quickly; but the effect of him was magical. Not only on the young men, who recovered themselves instantly from their easy attitudes and late-in-the-evening demeanour ; but Cordelia, suddenly mute and with cheeks hotly flaming, threw down her tambourine, sprang from her pedestal, and made as if she would have run away. His voice detained her as effectually as if he had seized her.

'I have come for you, Miss Ashby, so do not be in a hurry, but walk back with me, if you will so favour me.'

No answer ; but Cordelia stepped meekly by his side, the change from the smell of wine and tobacco to the fragrance of cedar and pine not more complete than that of her behaviour.

' Mrs. Wastel is going away ; you and Lettice and I are told off with her to the first Warren carriage. Do you know that although I have seen you several times I do not know yet whether you are a child or a grown-up young lady. I think I have been treating you as a child and from Aunt Susan's point of view, calling you Cordelia, as my cousins do ; and yet to-night you look older, and of a standing for more ceremony.'

No answer, and it is too dark to see her face ; but that drooping head suggests discouragement.

' Your unusual name is pleasant in the mouth, and as you are young enough for a doubt I shall claim the benefit of it, and say " Cordelia " as often as I find it musical.'

' Yes.'

' Perhaps it was the duty of one of those young men to escort you to the house, and I have clumsily taken you from your partner ? '

' Oh, *no* ; it is so *much* better to be with you ! '

' If I had known that I would have come sooner,' he answered, laughing at her emphasis.

' I—I am so ashamed—I ought not to have been singing like that ; I did *not* know it was wrong till I saw you.'

' Am I then so awful that folly dies at the sight of me ? '

' I never thought of it.   Those fellows were laughing, and their feeble minds are so soon astonished. Aunt Susan would not have liked it, would she ? '

' Very likely not. I hardly know what is thought becoming now for young ladies. Something depends on whether we are to consider you as a child, or as a responsible young woman.'

' I am seventeen and five months. Girls do all sorts of things, and nobody minds ; but I ought not to run rigs, because—I do not really care for larks, and only take them because there is nothing else yet ; but what I have come for is to learn to be very good, the really best kind of goodness. Will you teach me, Mr. Odiarne ? Will you show me how ? I have been thinking of it for a long time, and I have quite made up my mind, but I do not know the least thing about it—will you help me ? '

They had come now to the windows of the drawing-room ; the clergyman looked at the wild figure that turned round to him on the step in the light that shone on her from

within; he saw her strange dress, her rough
hair, her flushed face and eager eyes, and read
the strong appeal that entirely animated her as
she put up her hands and nearly, but not quite,
touched his arm, and repeated 'Teach me to
be good.' He was deeply stirred, for his professional instincts, very strong—for he was
clergyman to his finger-tips—his personal con-
victions, which were stronger still, and strongest
of all, his kind heart, all drew him to this sup-
pliant. There was a doubt, it is true, caused by
the perception that even he could not escape, of
the incongruity of her appearance and conduct
with her aspirations; but he was still more
conscious of a disinclination for the inevitable
boring and fuss that would come to him if he
undertook this task; and as this was unworthy
and must be checked, he answered the more
readily—

'My child, I will help you—if you will
remember that it is help only from a fellow-
learner.'

'Oh, thank you! You have promised; you will not forget!' said Cordelia, in soft triumph, and with a look of ecstasy. She went home from her first ball in absorbed silence, saying to herself, 'Now I shall begin. It will be all right; now I shall begin.'

CHAPTER XI.

STUMBLING-BLOCKS.

O who will show me those delights on high?
                    Echo . . . 'I.'
Thou, Echo, thou art mortall, all men know.

                                        G. Herbert.

THE next day Mrs. Wastel thought that inter-
views on the subject of Cordelia would never
cease.   Mayne was the first, begging that she
would keep her at the Warren a day or two
longer.   'We all like her, you know, and it
must be dull with Aunt Susan and the old
maids—besides, they will be glad of a little
peace.'

Mrs. Wastel fancied that her stepson was
not speaking all his thought, and her look
questioned him.

'That is not all.   I heard some fellows
speaking of her father with something a good

deal short of respect and esteem ; and perhaps if the girl goes about a little with you and Lettice, it will show that she is all right, and that we take her on her own account.'

' Thank you, Mayne. I am glad you told me. No harm can come of having her here ; but it would be greatly against my wish that her father should darken doors of yours or mine.'

' He does not seem an oppressively loving parent, and he will hardly affect this neighbourhood. If he should turn up he must be handed over to Aunt Susan. May I be there to see ! '

Lettice looked bright and fresh at breakfast, and explained that she did not allow going out in the evening to interfere with her duties next day ; Tuesday was one of her school mornings. Cordelia came down last, rather pale, and surprised to find even the gentlemen finishing their breakfast. 'I thought no one came down to breakfast after a dance ; I only

came now because Lettice was sure to be up;
and I met her going out.'

'You cannot do better than follow her
example in a good many things,' said Mrs.
Longley, tartly. 'How nice Lettice looked
last night, Mrs. Wastel, so ladylike and sweet.
Lettice has such nice manners, so quiet and
gentle; there is nothing fast and vulgar about
her, and you never hear her talking loudly or
see her making herself conspicuous in any way.'

'Here is some hot toast, Cordie. May I
cut you some ham, or is Sedley to be honoured
with your commands? I am so glad you are
late; Lettice is perfectly horrid the morning
after a ball,' said Mayne to his young guest,
whose colour was effectually restored by Mrs.
Longley's remarks.

'Have a brandy-and-soda, Miss Ashby.
Wastel has recommended it to me; it is my
belief that Sedley has had his in bed and Miss
Wastel hers overnight,' said Captain Longley,
who also wished to be kind.

'I was nine hours in my dress clothes,' moaned Mr. Sedley; 'how you ladies could stand it in your tight—well—things, I cannot tell.'

'At least, Miss Ashby wore nothing tight,' said Mrs. Longley, who did not join the laugh.

'Mind you never do, Cordie, or you will get a red nose,' said Mayne, making it worse with Mrs. Longley.

'I suppose you will have to speak to that young lady presently, Mrs. Wastel,' Mrs. Longley began in the course of their morning stroll. 'It is always a nuisance to have to take out strange girls; they are sure to vex you in some way.'

'I am not vexed with my young cousin; but I am vexed with myself for not making sure that she had a suitable dress for last night.'

'But her goings on all the evening—making an uproar at dinner, marching about independently, and never coming near you! You really ought to know that my husband heard she danced a hornpipe and sang to a lot of tipsy young men and all the servants down by the pavilion ! I know that is true, for I saw Mr. Odiarne bringing her back.'

' She is very young still, but she is not like the young bear, for so many of her troubles in the way of disadvantages are past that we may hope not many more lie before her,' said Mrs. Wastel, so gently that her gentleness was a reproof. ' When you come down at Christmas I hope you will find her quite toned down. We all think there is much very good material in her for the making of a noble woman. It is a fine natural character.'

Mrs. Longley burned to suggest that Mr. Wastel would be the most efficient tutor, and seemed well inclined for the office ; but she was awed. Her Harry was devoted to the Wastels, but she did not share his feeling, being embarrassed by a superiority that she had no desire to imitate. She contented herself with a meaning look at the portico where Cordelia stood in close conversation with Mayne.

' You are not going away to-day,' he was saying. 'Aunt Susan is delighted to be rid of you, and we are more delighted to keep you here.'

' As I don't believe about Aunt Susan, I can't believe about you. Do you know she kissed me before I came away on Saturday, and said " God bless you." No one ever said that to me before.' Cordelia's eyes were moist as she said this ; she did not guess that Mayne felt a little pinch at his heart, and relieved it by inwardly repeating Aunt Susan's benediction.

' It is nonsense to talk of going to-day ; you must stay.'

' Must ? ' Cordelia threw back her head and looked dangerous. Mayne remembered the manner of her arrival at Ivy Cottage.

' Stay to please us, Cordelia ; to please the mother and Lettice, not to speak of me. You know the mother insists on all the invitations being mine, so I have the pleasure of asking you.'

' I am not sure about Lettice ; she is angry with me.   But I should like to please you and my cousin, for I do not think you are saying it only for pretty. Mayne, will you tell me something, on your very faithful promise ? '

' Yes ; what is it ? '

' What did I do wrong last night.   I know I made an awful mull of it all.   Lettice is furious, and Mrs. Longley is like an angry black pigeon this morning—poo-oo-oo, poo-oo-oo.   Why are you not as tight and black as I am, poo-oo-oo ?   What was it ? '

' If I tell you, and you are angry with me, I shall think you shabby.'

' I am no sneak—go on.'

' Well, you know, you are not quite like the girls about here—and though it is not your fault——'

' It makes people lift up their eyebrows—so—and look at me up and down as you look at a horse that some one else has bought. And you would rather they did not, when I am in your crowd?'

'I am not too selfish about it, Cordie. I think you are much too nice a girl for any one to lift eyebrows at. Another time we must contrive that you do not dance with all the Maybury cads; but you need not trouble yourself about that, for they will not have another chance.'

'Were they cads? I am afraid I do not know many nice men; they were as good as most of the Colonel's little lot; and, of course, I did not expect them to be like you.' This compliment was said with an air of sorrowful gravity that quite prevented Mayne from showing that he appreciated it. Then, with a sudden enlightenment, she said, 'You do not know the worst thing I did last night?'

'The bull's eye in Miss Carling's champagne, you bad child?'

'That was nothing! but down at that

drinking-place I found a tambourine, and one of the cads asked me if I could sing—so I jumped on a post, and sang " Carlino." '

' And I was not there to see ! '

' Worse than that happened. Mr. Odiarne ! He came up with that look of his—you know, up above everything. I felt something like bad when I saw him. Once I did a worse thing than that, and on purpose, and I was marched back in the dark and scolded all the way; but I was not nearly so cut up. He did not scold one word; he hardly knew what I had been up to, and of course I felt all the greater wretch.'

' What did you say to him ? ' asked Mayne, yielding to the vice of curiosity.

' I asked him if he would teach me to be very good. He actually said he would, and never laughed at me. I have always wanted to go in for that kind of thing ; now I can begin at last ! That is why I want to go back to Ivy Cottage.'

' No one can help you better than Philip ;

but you will not lose time by staying here this week. We have a garden-party to-morrow, and he will most likely come up; only you know you cannot hold high talk over the tea and tennis-balls.'

'I shall give up all those things.'

'Not at Philip's bidding, since he takes most of his own recreation that way. Now, go and make it up with Lettice; I must be off to the workhouse.'

Lettice had consulted her mother in dire perplexity. The difficulty must be unusual that made Lettice consult her mother; though she loved her heartily, and was a fairly dutiful daughter to her, she was not the first of her admirers. 'Mother is so sentimental, and has so many considerations; she never goes straight at a thing,' was her verdict; and she could not understand the influence Mrs. Wastel exerted.

'What am I to do with Cordelia, mother? She is so slippery and contradictory that I do not know what to make of her. She is always talking of being good, till I really thought she meant it. On Sunday, particularly, when she wished to come to school with me, and seemed to take to it. I saw her listening with all her might in church.'

'So did I. Poor child, I prayed for her then. When we think of the hopelessness of her surroundings hitherto, it seems as if she were specially led towards a higher life; we are too apt to think it a mere result of training.'

'But can she be in earnest? Just look at her behaviour since! I tried to talk seriously to her after that, but she slipped away from me as usual; so I thought perhaps Philip might suit her better, and asked him to see to her; then, the very next night, she behaves in such a way! Philip will think I am a proper goose.'

'And you can never bear to be thought mistaken; but I do not think you are far wrong this time.'

'But last night, mother! She was disgraceful! I was so ashamed of her; and Mayne had to dance with her!'

'She was trying, certainly; but a good deal can easily be mended, and a good deal more will mend itself. It is not in the power of a girl like that to disgrace your brother, nor you either. For her mother's sake, or rather for mine, I must ask you to be patient with her. Do not try too hard to do her good yourself, but just be friendly and companionable. I am asking it as a favour, Lettice.'

'Oh, don't make so much of it as that, mother! She must behave decently, and I will try her again.'

The two girls settled their difference; Lettice being again surprised by Cordelia's change of tone, and receiving her penitence with great kindness. She even offered further guidance, which Cordelia again declined.

At the Warren garden-party Cordelia was almost too exemplary—eschewing the society of the young and frivolous, and devoting herself

to Aunt Susan, who had come up for this her
one gaiety, and sat on the terrace, looking like
an old fairy, with her bright eyes and curly
hair, with her crutch-handled stick and black
satin cloak. Jock Somers was particularly
anxious to make up for lost time in his acquaintance with Cordelia; but he was disappointed,
for Tim and Toby had given a vivid sketch of
the fun to be got out of her, and the decorous
figure in dark blue and a hat that Lettice had
perhaps too vigorously reformed, did little to
recall the gay and festive young person of
yesternight.

'If you won't play tennis, come and have a
shy at " Aunt Sally."'

'Aunt Susan is my only joy!'

'She does not want you,' said Jock; 'don't
you see she is carrying on with my father. She
is the only person here who was not at our kick-
up the other day, and so she is very interesting
to the dear old boy, for he can fully describe it
to her.'

This was so obvious that Cordelia went to the seats overlooking the tennis-court, whither Jock followed. 'I am afraid you find this sort of thing desperately slow; but in the country, you know, we cannot get up a dance, or theatricals, or any kind of lark more than once in three months.'

'Oh, no! that is not why I cannot play these games. I am going to do something different, and I shall give up jolly dogs and all sorts of sprees.'

'Oh, I say, Miss Ashby! Are you going into a convent, or—or something of that sort?'

'I do not know. I may have to do it; but good people do not always.'

'I should think not! Lettice is the best girl I know, and she does not look like a convent, does she?'

'Not just now.' Lettice was making a vigorous rally at tennis against a tough opponent, and both Cordelia and Jock paused to admire and then applaud her.

' Now, Miss Ashby, you agree it is possible to be good and play tennis too ? '

' Of course it is ; did I say it was not, you particularly stupid young man ? ' and Cordelia told him about the project for a new tennis-lawn, and the way in which Mayne and Lettice gave it up. She was rather disappointed that Jock took it as a matter of course.

A little later, Mr. Odiarne—a tall black figure between the shorter white ones of Mayne and Tim Somers—came to where Cordelia was sitting, on a grassy bank, a little apart from the rest. She received them with a fine red blush, that Tim, sage youth, thought must be on Mayne's account. Mayne thought it proceeded from twinges of conscience at sight of Tim. Mr. Odiarne did not notice it at all ; he was so much away from and above the region of small things that his observation was not very quick. Finding that Cordelia would not play tennis, Mayne carried off Tim and left her to the Vicar.

' Well, Cordelia, what are your morning

thoughts? Do you still hold me to my promise of the other night?'

Cordelia's face glowed assent, but she said nothing. Mr. Odiarne sat down by her on the bank.

'I should laugh at one of my curates if he were to begin professionally on a young lady at a garden-party; but I am old enough for exceptions, and there is no time like the present. Lettice would approve of that sentiment.'

'Yes, she always begins at once.'

'Ah! not many people have such a well-regulated mind as Lettice, or, if they begin with it, they do not keep it to double her age. Tell me something of your history—what you know, what you like, and what you want to know.'

'I have learnt very nearly nothing.'

'Whose fault has that been—yours?'

Cordelia told her little tale of neglect and loneliness, of her desultory life and utter lack of training and sweet influences, not knowing how pathetic it seemed to her hearer.

'Now tell me what and whom you like. I want to know the favourable side of you.'

'I love Aunt Susan dearly, and Mrs. Wastel. I like Mayne and Lettice ; Miss Carling, too, a little, though she is rather an odd bird.'

'That is good, especially Aunt Susan. Any one would like the others, but she is of the nature of salt. A child or a foolish person might find the taste of her a little sharp ; but she is one of the indispensable, the savour of all things. But who were your friends before you came here ?'

'I care very much for Fero, my sister Sophy's boy. He is not like her, but such a darling ! I like George Kingdon too, one of the Mentone crowd ; he is a baddish lot, I am afraid, but he is always chummy with me. Sœur Lucie is the person I have always thought most of. Do you think it is wicked to love a Romanist? She is quite too awfully good, and I want to be like her, if you can show me how.' And Cordelia, warming into slang, told her new friend of the saint-like sister who had influenced her so strongly. Then a few more questions sounded the depth of her own personal negligences and ignorances, told with a freedom and candour to which Mr. Odiarne was unaccustomed.

'In a few days I will give you some books, and something to learn by heart; I am going to treat you as a child, a little step backward will not hurt you. You had better attend a class that Mr. Knox holds for girls.'

'I would rather you taught me.'

'I am going to teach you—a little submission.'

'To learn as you think fit? Well—yes, I will do it. When am I to begin?'

'I will give you one thing to begin on at once, as I see you wish that. It is to speak always respectfully of your father.'

'How can I if I do not respect him, and how can I respect him if he is an old——'

'Hush!' Mr. Odiarne looked so stern that his pupil felt more awe than she had experienced before human being up to that hour. Of course she admired him in proportion, and listened reverently to his very short enforcement of the principle of the fifth commandment, which, as the first moral lesson she had ever set herself seriously to apply, opened to her the enormous, the life-long difficulty of the step that lies between knowing and doing.

'Thank you, Cousin Philip; you are the very best man in the world!' whispered Lettice, when they were all standing about the tea-table, and Cordelia was carrying queen-cakes to Aunt Susan.

'Very much so, indeed,' answered the Vicar, grimly; 'and your cousin Cordelia is the best young woman in the world; so I beg that you will treat her as such, and neither try to teach

her anything, nor let her think herself interest-
ingly wicked.'

'Very well; but you had better warn
Mayne too about the last, for that is just what
he thinks her,' returned Lettice, with a grain
of malice, and not sorry to see the Vicar look
discomfited.

CHAPTER XII.

MORE ZEAL THAN DISCRETION.

Ye holy men, so earnest in your care,
Of your own mighty instruments beware!
Wordsworth.

'DEAREST, sweetest, loveliest Aunt Susan! how perfectly delicious it is to come back to you and to Ivy Cottage, and to the old maids and home! I must call it home; you don't mind, do you? And oh, Aunt Susan! such a beautiful thing has happened to me, and I am to have my great wish!'

Cordelia paused, not from want of words, but to give her news due effect. Miss Hooper settled her cap, recovered her newspaper, and pretended to be very much fussed by her great-niece's sudden entrance. 'My dear! we did not know you were coming this afternoon. Tell French at once, so that there may be cakes for tea ; and stop, my dear, Andrew will take your box upstairs.'

'Oh, my box! I dare say it will come when they send for the second post. Never mind that, my dearest dear. I want to tell you my good news!'

Aunt Susan looked at her anxiously. She was not such a child after all ; she seemed to have grown older in these last ten days ; and you can never depend on young men, even such as Mayne ; and how very awkward it would be if there should be anything—Colonel Ashby such a very undesirable connection! The child seemed quite excited. Miss Hooper's heart stood still as Cordelia went on, with one of her biggest blushes too.

'Only think what a splendid thing for me! What I have been longing, and trying, and scheming for, and now it seems too good to be true! Mr. Odiarne, his very own self, is going to teach me to be good—very good; of the same kind of goodness as his own! Is it not frightfully good of him, when I have just been running such rigs?'

'Is that all, my dear? You quite frightened me. I am glad to hear it; and it is very kind of the Vicar. But you must not be a charge on his time; you know he has all the parish to teach.'

'Yes, but I am to learn something special. I think it is called the higher life.'

'If you mean a Christian life, nothing can be higher than that; and he wishes all his people to lead it.' Aunt Susan spoke tartly.

'And do they?'

'If they do not, there is no excuse for them. No one in Maybury can plead that they have not both teaching and example.'

'But are they better?'

'Indeed I think so. A great many are following his lead, and the young people are especially touched; but Mr. Odiarne himself is always anxious that we should not try to count converts, to separate wheat from tares, or to estimate what is necessarily unseen by line and rule. I can say for myself that I have learned much from this young man, although I thought I knew all about it before he was born.'

'Do you call Mr. Odiarne a young man?'

'He is not much more than forty-five. That is young in my old eyes.'

'Forty! that is quite old. I am glad of that, for I do not think young men can teach one, do you?'

'They always think they can, so perhaps they are right sometimes.'

Cordelia turned over her new leaf with a good deal of rustle and flutter. She fairly chattered about Mr. Odiarne, his likes and dislikes, his goings and comings, his sermons, and even his lessons to her. Aunt Susan rather enjoyed hearing all this, and did not check her. Lettice was contemptuous, and set her cousin down for a fool, and Cordelia would not take advice from her in consequence. Then Mrs. Wastel interfered, and Cordelia promised to obey, but could not understand, and it was not advisable to damp her by telling her that she was unduly and unwholesomely excited.

'You love all sorts of goodness and of good people, and you often speak of these things,' she said one day, when Mrs. Wastel was trying to tone her down a little.

' Yes ; but I do not speak at all times nor to every one. Then I am so much older than you are, graver too, as becomes my years and what has come to pass in them. I am more established, as it were, and my surroundings are oftener in tune with high subjects than yours can be. I do not sit on the hall table in a Tam-o'-Shanter cap to-day to explain the views on baptismal regeneration that I learnt yesterday, as I saw some one doing this morning. My friends are older than yours, and many of them think with me. If you listen a little you will find that we indulge in these topics rarely, and only when we are sure of being all of one mind on great matters. You made me very hot the other day at luncheon by talking to Mr. Merridew about instantaneous conversion when Mr. Stepney was there, who calls himself an agnostic. Now Mr. Stepney is a thoughtful person whom I much respect, and think very much better than his opinions. We often have a little discussion on them when no one is listening, and he is always very careful not to drop a word that may offend me. Judge of my feelings when I heard you making yourself ridiculous on the gravest matters, of which you cannot possibly understand all the bearings.'

'I am sorry, cousin. I saw Mr. Merridew did not like it; but I thought he was ashamed of goodness and of being a parson.'

'Not he! He was ashamed of your want of tact, and afterwards begged my pardon for your fault.'

'Did he? How first-rate of him; he is not half bad! But, cousin, I often hear you and Aunt Susan and Mr. Odiarne say things that make one see and think of the very best things.'

' Do you ? I am glad of that. My aunt is an old-fashioned Christian, of a pattern that is often thought cold and hard, severely respectable, and wanting in enthusiasm and sympathy, therefore often failing to exert a wide influence; but she has all the virtues of her school, and few of its failings. She is so clear and upright, as well as so kindly, that she is a tower of strength to those who do not find her too rugged and grim.'

' And you, cousin ? '

' I humbly trust that I have the root of the matter ; but I am like a climbing plant, with little strength of my own, and I lean on any one who has more firmness than I have. My way is to sentimentalise too much, to lean too much to the side of feeling, to over-refine, and so lose the clearness and honesty of mind and soul that, next to a hearty desire for goodness, are perhaps the most essential to real progress.'

'But is not speaking out the most honest way? And how is one to learn and to understand people if one does not talk of these things?'

'In one way, the way of observation, you can learn from every one; but observation means silence. As to words, it is surprising how few people teach one anything directly. Then you know these matters are the very core of the heart; very few like to speak of them at all; there is a feeling that there is a lack of modesty and reserve in proclaiming the deep and secret workings of God in the soul before the multitude; it is the grace of spiritual shyness. I should greatly doubt any older person whom I saw to be without it. And for you, I think it will develop as you understand better. Philip Odiarne is an appointed teacher; yet how cautious he is in his dealing with deep subjects!'

'One cannot imagine him less than perfection!'

'He would not say so; and though he has his weaknesses, it is not necessary for you to look for them. He has the gift of a singularly pure and noble nature. This is, as it were, a vantage ground for him; he is called, in an especial manner, to be a saint; and it seems to be required of him that he should attain to lofty heights of goodness, and raise others with him. He impressed me in this way when I first knew him; yet I can see—feel, rather— that he has advanced much in these fifteen years. His spiritual life has become both deeper and higher.'

'Fifteen years! Has it taken him so long to be so good?'

'Longer than that; more than forty. He has from his baptism lived the rest of his life according to that beginning. What we see is the growth in grace, "shining ever more unto the perfect day." Fifteen years is as nothing in such a life—a life that is not mortal, but immortal; it takes long enough to understand it from the outside, to see it in all its bearings.'

'You say that nature is a gift. Do you mean that some people are born with it, a fairy gift of goodness, so that they cannot help it?'

'It is God's gift, most truly, and a very rare and precious one. Some people do seem, as you say, born with it; the qualities are in some measure hereditary, and it is part of the blessing on the children of the righteous. Colonel Odiarne, Philip's father, an excellent officer, who distinguished himself in active service in India, was a man who exerted a strong influence for good in his regiment, at a time when to lead a Christian life under such circumstances was to suffer a very real persecution.'

'There would have been a chance for me if I had been the daughter of *that* Colonel,' said Cordelia, with a sigh, which made Mrs. Wastel wish she had not taken her moralising quite so far.

'We are speaking of an especial and singular gift, you know. If our talents are but two, or one, they must be used.'

'I mean to be something very special. It will be all the harder if it is not in me, as it is in Sœur Lucie and Mr. Odiarne.'

Cordelia took some warning about promiscuous talking; but she did not yet, nor all at once, attain the grace of spiritual modesty and reserve, not until she began to feel the real stress of the spiritual conflict for which as yet she was only storing the weapons.

Mr. Odiarne did not bestow much time on his pupil, but he gave her some books and directions for studying them, with some instruction and advice as to private devotion, and he put her in the way of learning what was taught in the Maybury Sunday schools to the elder children. She would have thriven better on the lessons to the little ones, so destitute was she of the usual teaching; but her good will to learn stood her in good stead, and Mr. Odiarne, though he might only talk to her for a few minutes at long intervals, allowed her to feel that she was his own pupil and special care. No more than this was needed to keep her constantly eager, and at the full stretch of her powers. He was amazed at her capacity for learning, and refreshed and encouraged by her intense devotion to her subject, so different from the childish, unwilling, or indifferent minds that formed so large a proportion of those he had to teach. This made her a most attractive pupil, and her master built up a fair scheme of rapid and noble development for this fresh and ready hearer, who seemed to present no opposing force to the pure and exalted conception of Christianity that he strove to put before her. Insensibly led by her untiring attention and ready comprehension, he went on from the truths and doctrines to his own meditations and reflections on them, and would try the effect of some personal view, some new thought, some private speculation, upon her receptive mind. It seemed to matter little what he said, in one way, for Cordelia drank in everything, classic or original, with the same avidity and perfect faith in him, though she constantly disregarded his warnings as to what might not be fully thought out, or a matter on which there were grave differences of opinion, or a thought that had only crossed his mind at the moment of speaking.

Finding that Cordelia's ignorance of the letter of Scripture greatly impeded her understanding of his illustrations, the Vicar begged her to attend a Bible class for young women, held weekly by the senior curate, Mr. Knox. Here she was not exemplary ; she made light of Mr. Knox, chiefly because he was not Mr. Odiarne; he had a small rasping voice, and a dry manner, which she would not forgive, even when she began to share the interest his other pupils found in their work.

' What have you been teaching Miss Ashby

on the theory of prophecy?' asked Mr. Knox of his chief.

'I? nothing; not much at least. Why do you ask?'

'She said something so odd yesterday about the visions of Ezekiel, I could not tell what she was driving at; but she quoted you with much confidence, and I suppose she had taken hold of something you said wrong way first— women always do,' said the much tried little man.

'Does she ask questions?' inquired the Vicar, who was at one with him as touching women in general.

'I allow questions at the end of the lecture only, otherwise I cannot keep these young persons at all to the point; allow one to speak, and the conversation immediately becomes general. Miss Ashby does not so much ask questions, as give us all instruction in your name. She said something about the eagles and the vine, and the highest branch. I think it was to the effect that some people were the favoured ones, the higher branches, and so more acceptable. I confess I do not see all the bearings of the passage myself, and I did not attempt to answer her.'

'I think I was building up a theory of spiritual aspiration, and of the glorious ambition of those who would win a special crown, and press forward to the farthest mark.'

' Is that milk for babes ? '

'I hardly look on her as such ; she is capable of receiving a great deal,' said the Vicar, with a shade of apology in his tone.

'She does not yet thoroughly know the Catechism.'

'Very likely, she does not submit herself to her spiritual pastors. However, she can apprehend the truths without the form of words.'

'The form of words is a very serviceable anchor : I have bidden her learn her " duty to her neighbour," as well as the kings of Israel and Judah.'

'Very good. You are a better teacher of youth than I am, Knox.'

'Not so. You are professor in a higher school than I; but in this case your disciple has not first graduated in the lower one, as is the wholesome custom.'

About this time, Cordelia wrote a letter—so rare an occurrence, that Miss Hooper, seeing her busy with pen and ink, looking hot, and with her hair rumpled, asked if she were writing to her father.

'Oh no, he knows where I am, and does not want reminding of me. I am writing to George Kingdon. Do not you think it is a pity to put in commas, they spoil the effect if you get them in the wrong places?'

'But you must learn to put them in the right places; it is a mark of a gentlewoman that her letter is rightly punctuated.'

'George thinks me a cad, to begin with, and I don't believe he knows much about stops himself.'

' Is it necessary to write to such a person ? '

'Yes; he is rather a shady lot, but he is a gentleman, and thinks it very poor form not to keep promises.'

'My dear! can you have anything to say to make it needful to write to a doubtful character ? '

' It is all right, Aunt Susan. I am only telling him what a good thing it is for me to have hopped across Mr. Odiarne.'

Miss Hooper was divided between her duty as in charge of her niece and her delicate feelings about other people's letters. As she pondered, Cordelia came to an end, with only one more difficulty.

' Ought I to say " yours sincerely " or " truly "? '

'As you write to a gentleman, " truly " will be better, I think.'

' Easier to spell, that decides it ! ' and Cordelia read over her letter with modest satisfaction.

'DEAR GEORGE,—I promised to tell you
when I found any one to teach me how to be
very good. So here I am. It is Mr. Odiarne,
the Vicar here; he is quite tremendously good
—the best man I ever met—bar none. There
is no question of laughing at or chaffing him, I
can tell you. I hope soon to be very religious,
and wish you would learn the same—there is
nothing like it, as I told you. The people here
are all good, and very jolly too.

'Yours truly,

'CORDELIA ASHBY.'

Miss Hooper's cogitations led her to propose
that Cordelia should have a morning governess
for a few weeks. She propounded the plan
diffidently.

'Will she teach me about the commas, and
the meaning of words in the Bible, or will she
bother with German declensions and the history
of British India?' asked Cordelia, cautiously.

'She shall teach you the things in which

you feel most deficient.   I hardly know what is taught now.   I learnt grammar and geography, ciphering and the use of the globes; your mother learnt arithmetic and Italian and chemistry; Lettice learnt mathematics and physiology and German and Latin.'

' Oh dear, I shall never rise to that.   Had I not better learn reading and writing, and all the little things that everybody knows ? '

' Yes, indeed, my dear.   Miss Spenser, who has been a governess and is a superior young person, is obliged now to live with her mother, who thinks herself a great invalid ; I do not know what her complaint is, but she requires attention.   We will enquire about Miss Spenser to-morrow.'

So Cordelia spent the long summer mornings in patching up her rickety education. The restraint galled her, but she submitted bravely for the most part, only taking an occasional break out. Mrs. Wastel advised an easy rule, lessons in the garden, a good deal of talking, or

conversation lessons, as Miss Spenser preferred
to call them, and by a happy hit, some his-
torical novels—Scott, James, Bulwer, and Miss
Yonge—with all the educational side-lights to
be thrown on them by maps and dictionaries.
Miss Spenser proved sensible; but she chiefly
gained her pupil's respect by confessing herself
an ardent admirer and disciple of Mr. Odiarne,
and her attention by going over his lectures
and sermons so as to teach Cordelia the important lessons of how to learn and how to
listen.

CHAPTER XIII.

A LOOK BACKWARD.

Thou standest in the rising sun,
And in the setting thou art fair.

Tennyson.

ONE morning Mr. Odiarne was walking to the Uplands on some pastoral business. His passage through the town was constantly interrupted ; a word from the doctor about a patient, then a great many from a district visitor about a naughty girl. Then a woman—her sister's husband had beaten his wife, and wasn't drunk either—would the Vicar see about it? Then his eye fell on a small girl ; being a practised eye, it distinguished her from seven or eight other small girls with whom she was importantly marching home from the infant school.

'Amelia Barnes, why does not your sister come to school now ? '

Amelia's fat face looked very wise; being a
trained infant, she spoke up distinctly from the
height of the Vicar's knee—

'She ain't coming to big school no more.
She goes to Methodist.'

'Indeed! And does she like that?'

'Oh-h, yes. She likes it; they give her
two apples every day, and sixpence for going!'

Next came an old woman in great grief.

'Pig doyed last night. Took bad, he was.
We fetched him in to the fire and wrapped him
up in the blanket; but 'twarn't no use, he
wouldn't stop!'

Of another old woman Mr. Odiarne asked
after her son who had gone for a soldier.

'He be getting along very well, thank *you*,
sir. He be got among the " awls "; he be
either a generawl or a corporawl, I don't rightly
know which, but it be among the " awls." '

The day was very hot, and, coming out of
the town, the Vicar kept under the shadow of
the wall, topped by a hedge, that bounded Miss

Hooper's garden. In this hedge grew a far-spreading yew-tree, very accessible from the garden side, but some height above the green border of the highway. There was a great rustle and creak in this tree as he came near, and Cordelia Ashby swung herself down from the branches just before him.

'I have startled you, Mr. Odiarne! You did not know I could get through this tree!'

'I did not know that you would; and I did not know you wore red stockings.'

Cordelia's face matched her stockings. 'I am always doing wrong things, and only finding them out when you look at me. I saw you coming, and thought I would ask you about the sins of the fathers being visited on the children. What does it mean?'

'George Luck got drunk and fell over the cradle; the baby was hurt and will always be lame.'

'Poor baby! What a shame! I am the worse for the Colonel's little ways, and because

he spends the money on himself that ought
to have gone for my schooling. Is that what
you want to say?'

'What is Miss Spenser doing?'

'Eating raspberries, finding the places in
the map of Spain that are mentioned in the
"Conquest of Granada," and wondering what
has become of me.'

'Now I am going to speak very plainly to
you; and as Miss Spenser has the raspberries, you
may walk up the hill with me. You remember
what I said to you about honouring your father
and mother?'

'Yes. I have done as you told me about
him—the prayers. How surprised he would be
if he knew! It is no trouble to honour poor
mamma in my thoughts. I always think of her
as so beautiful and unhappy.'

'Her story is a very sad one; and, though it
must give you pain, I think it will be good for
you to hear it. Aunt Susan gave me leave,
and you can ask her for the details. She was,

as you say, very beautiful; and she was unhappy, for she spoilt her own life. She had a great power of attracting strong love; her father must have idolised her; Aunt Susan and Mrs. Wastel deeply love her still, and they love you for her sake—there you get the benefit of her best and most lovable qualities. But there is another side—she was not dutiful, she did not honour her father, nor trust him; possibly she only found out too late how much she loved him. Cordelia, she broke his heart by leaving her home secretly and running away to marry your father!'

'Oh, Mr. Odiarne!'

It was a severe blow. Cordelia blushed and gasped as she looked blankly at the kind face of her friend, and, reading many unsaid things there, she looked down blushing again, and two large tears rolled down her cheeks for the pity of it, of that long ago sin.

'It must be pain to you, poor child. I wished you to be told sooner, for you were sure to hear it some day. You know I would not wilfully grieve you,' said the Vicar, very gently, and Cordelia presently looked up again ; nothing could be too grievous when he seemed grieved for her and spoke with such kindness ; he had something to say too, and she must listen. ' Now, think of this: every wilful lawless thing you do, every carelessness of speech or behaviour, reflects back on your mother as well as on your father. Here are people to say, "That was her mother's spirit," and to recollect her conduct with more harshness than they otherwise would. On the other hand, if you are dutiful and gentle, a good woman and a gentlewoman, there are others, far better and more worthy of being heeded, who will say, " Her mother was very sweet ; she is like her, and reminds us of all the best of her." More than this—your shortcomings may be part of her punishment ; they certainly would have been had she lived— or rather, she now sees her own in the light of eternity, she measures them by the height and

depth and agony of her forgiveness.   And you,
her daughter, you must live with both sides of
her example before you, yet referring all to the
great Example.'

Cordelia did not speak, but she looked her
acceptance of this, and Mr. Odiarne went on:
'See now, here, in her own place, you more
than any one may honour her memory; and if
you begin to do that rightly, you will learn
how to forgive and honour your father too. It
is hard for you, but it must be done. Begin
with a little outward sign—do not call him
"the Colonel" any more; say "my father";
then you must needs remember the Father of
Whom both you and he are erring children.'

He stopped and bade her good-bye, sug-
gesting an excuse to Miss Spenser. Cordelia
dashed down the hill and into her own room.
Miss Spenser did not see her eccentric pupil at
all that day; on the next, 'Mr. Odiarne was
talking to me,' was ample reason for the defec-
tion, and from that time the governess found

her, if not always docile and attentive, at least seriously anxious to be so.

Miss Hooper believed herself to spend Sunday in extreme quiet and repose. Really, it was the busiest day of her week. She wore her best gown, which was in itself exciting; she drove with much state and ceremony to Maybury Church, where, though the seats were strictly free and unappropriated, she would have been much surprised to miss her usual chair. The Vicar and churchwardens winked at this indulgence, declaring that for no one but Miss Hooper would other people submit to the monopoly.

To Cordelia these Sundays became a deep excitement. She was learning to follow the services, and to fix her unaccustomed attention, enlarging her capacity for devotion by slow degrees. Meanings began to unfold for her here and there, and her bright intelligence applied well what was taught her; but when it was a question of matters in which Mr. Odiarne

had personally instructed her, she fastened on
them eagerly, with a flash of her spirit and a
glow of her heart that seemed to burn them in.
Surely it was the pure love of God that made
her feel thus — so lifted out of herself, so
radiantly happy in all good things? When the
Vicar preached she sat in rapt attention, her
whole soul bent to understand; and when he,
rising beyond eloquence, poured out his soul in
warm inspiration, she was the first to feel it, to
sit with bowed head and fast-dropping tears; or,
kindling quick at his enthusiasm, her hot young
heart would burn within her, she knew not
why; nor did she think it strange or perilous
that only one voice would move her so, that
only one utterance she received as a real message to herself—for was not this her chosen
teacher?

There was a custom at Maybury that on
Sundays the clergyman who went to the Uplands
for morning service came afterwards to Ivy
Cottage for luncheon, saving time and walking

before he went to another outlying hamlet.
Aunt Susan always apologised for the plain
meal that such old-fashioned people as herself
thought befitting the day of rest to the man-
servant and the maid-servant, and no one
thought it advisable to point out that it was
the daintiest meal of the week. Mr. Merridew,
the junior curate, much appreciated Cordelia,
who in turn liked him; he was a cheery boyish
creature, hearty both at work and play, and
giving good promise for the future in his present rather raw undevelopment. He was a
little afraid of Aunt Susan, who could not forgive his youth nor forget his great-uncles—
venerable friends of hers who died of old age
before their great-nephew was born. He found
Cordelia a welcome relief from the *tête-à-tête*
luncheons, and was extremely disconcerted
when Miss Hooper saw this, and told him so as
a mere matter of observation. Mr. Knox was
much more staid and dry; he was excellent,
but entirely professional. ' It is lucky that he

chiefly comes on Sundays; I should not know what to say to him on a week-day,' said Aunt Susan. As it was, they talked of Church and Dissent, old women and temperance societies. There was high *fête* at Ivy Cottage when the Vicar came; but this was rare.

A Sunday seldom passed without a visit from some of the Warren party on their way to or from Maybury Church. Mrs. Wastel would rest and talk, while Lettice walked about the garden with Cordelia, and Mayne inspected the pigs and the pony, and prescribed for Aunt Susan's fruit and rose trees. It happened about the time of Cordelia's receiving the above lecture that Mayne Wastel was away from home for a fortnight, 'between hay and harvest,' as he said in his character of British farmer, and also that he had not met Cordelia for some days after his return. Coming in alone one Sunday to the Ivy Cottage luncheon, he watched Cordelia and Mr. Merridew while he talked to Aunt Susan; and afterwards going with the younger lady to the kitchen garden, he observed, 'So they have tamed you, Cordelia?' Mr. Odiarne was not the only person who found Miss Ashby's Christian name pleasant on the tongue.

'They are trying; and so am I. Do you think I get on?'

'Only too fast. There is a change in you, my young friend. You have a caught and combed look; your gown is the most correct and fashionable imitation of a bottle; and you have done something to your hair, or is it a wig?'

'A wig; an old one of Mrs. Peabody's.'

'I thought bay was her colour. But this is not all; why is this gentle melancholy, this subdued light, this touching dignity? Above all, where are the picturesque expressions? I have not heard one all the morning.'

'I am trying to leave off. Is it slang to say a thing is a rummy go, when it is—well, very rummy, you know?'

'Some people would think so. So much depends on whom you speak to. I would not, if I were you, say it to Lady Somers; Merridew might forgive you. It would sound very stuck-up if you always spoke like a book; only cads, prigs, and cultured Americans do that—people whose gentility is so nicely balanced that it would be overset by a word not according to Cocker. I do not approve of the girl who said to her mother, " Now, old gal, let's be toddling ; " but if she had said " My honoured parent, my mind misgives me lest further delay should cause inconvenience," I should not like her much better.'

'You do not help me. I am trying so hard to get up a little behaviour, but you like to be able to laugh at me for being outrageous.'

'Not quite such a brute as that,' said Mayne, shortly, and with a flash that let Cordelia into secrets. This was not a man after George Kingdon's pattern, caring not what was thought of him; he was incapable of the mean-ness, and did not like to be accused of it. He went on in a different tone. 'What hum-bug it is, trying to make you flat and prim, and all sorts of things that are not the least in your style.'

'I am " thoroughly bad style," you know.'

'That is Mrs. Longley; never mind her. Are they not bearing too hard on you, Cordie; too much curb? You might tell me.'

Cordelia looked the other way, and her voice shook a little as she began, 'Don't you like me in this gown; it is new, and very much the thing; now you say it—it is like a bottle,' and she considered gravely the smooth dark-green surface.

'I do not think much of the gown, one way or other. I like you in it immensely; it is a pity there is not a button-hole some-where about it, this yellowish rose would make a good arrangement; it is " Marie van Houtte." '

Cordelia put out her hand for the rose, and pinned it under her chin.

'Did you ever try to be very good, Mayne? I thought it would be as easy as fun, when once I had made up my mind to go in for it; I meant it, and thought I could do as I please; it is very strange that one cannot. What do you make of it?'

'Not much. The fact is, that it is collar work all the way, and one must put one's heart into it, like a willing horse. I try after a fashion, for I know well enough that down hill leads to the deuce. You are good for a strong pull, Cordie, and—well, the coach is never quite too heavy.'

Mayne coloured, even through his summer complexion; Cordelia was beginning to know what it was to be shy, but she was hardly able to appreciate what this confession cost her friend.

'I should scorn to mind about giving up pleasant things—dancing, nice clothes, good-to-eat, and even jokes; but Mr. Odiarne does not want anything of that sort; he says I am to rule myself before I rule the world.'

'Is Philip too heavy on you? He has always kept himself in such strict order that he does not know how hard it is for happy-go-lucky people like you and me.'

'Oh, no. He is just perfect, and knows all about one better than oneself,' she said, with a heavy sigh.

That Sunday evening Cordelia stretched herself on the hearthrug at her aunt's feet, saying, 'Aunt Susan, will you tell me all you know about my mother? All, please, good and bad together.'

'My dear, I have wished to tell you. Truth is best, and truth will so far prevail that I do not fear you will love her less if I must tell you some things that are not good. But it always pains me to speak of her, and I cannot do it while you lie on the floor like that.'

'I beg your pardon! I wish I had learnt

manners; they are harder to make up than spelling even. Will this do, on the footstool under your elbow? Auntie, I have heard the worst of her—that she ran away, but I want to know how it came about.'

Miss Hooper told Rosina's story much as she told it to Mr. Odiarne before Cordelia came, but with a wonderful difference in her own feelings. Rosina's child had warmed her heart in her old age, and taken away some of the sting of Rosina's misdeeds; Cordelia had come to her with a message of love and penitence from the dead. Her hearer said little, until she heard of the deceit and the elopement; then she was roused.

' She must have been a horrid girl to serve you so! I cannot help feeling it, for it seems as if you were telling of a girl like me, not of my mother. It was mean, it was sneaky of her—and stupid too, to fancy any one could be better to her than you and Mrs. Wastel. To be sure, my father, when he likes, can persuade a horse's hind-leg off, and I dare say she thought he was quite a trump-card.'

'Cordelia, do not talk your slang about this! It sounds hateful to me.'

'Dearest! I am so sorry ; I forget sometimes, and sometimes I do not know the right words.'

'Yes. Rosina had been so carefully guarded that she really did not know a bad man when she saw him—ahem—I mean that she had no experience of various characters ; still she knew better than that, she must have known that she was doing very, very wrong.'

'And think what she must have felt when she found out the Colonel's little ways—I mean, that my father was not what she expected!'

'I am sure that when she came to herself she would struggle to make the best of him— for love, as you must do for duty, my child.'

'Mr. Odiarne said so. I wonder what he would say if he knew him. Auntie, it is as if you told me of a stranger, not of the mother I have always fancied. It is hard to forgive her for having hurt you so.' Cordelia kissed the square and faded hand that rested near to her on the crutch-handled stick.

'It was because we loved her so much that she hurt us so deeply. We spoilt her, and made her the centre of our lives ; she fancied the world was made for her to take what she liked out of.'

'And she took him! Oh, ye powers ! ' murmured the Colonel's daughter.

'You are not very like her, Cordelia. She was smaller and fairer, and very dainty and pretty in all her ways and manners; but you have a better temper, and a more unselfish and affectionate nature. One sees those things later— too late—and all the mistakes. God forgive us ! Remember, my dear, when you bear a grudge, as I fear you do, against your father for his neglect of you, that although it has been bad for your manners and ladylike training, yet it may have been better for you than spoiling. I could hardly have borne to trace your mother's failings in you, and so find new cause for self-reproach. So I love my big, awkward, truth-telling Cordelia, without too sore a heart about my poor darling, our broken idol.'

'And what about my father?' asked Cordelia, after a silence.

'My dear, you must ask Philip Odiarne about him, not me,' replied Aunt Susan, quite restored to her usual crispness.

CHAPTER XIV.

A MEETING.

. . . Those blind motions of the spring,
That show the year is turn'd.

Tennyson.

'THE Sandbay regatta is to be on Thursday, my lady ; if the Somerses will come I will drive you all in the break,' said Mayne Wastel to his stepmother.

'Very good. I will write to Silverwood. How many can you take?'

'We will drive Cocktail and the Grey ; they will pull eight easily. Toby is after grouse ; so there will be Jock and Tim, with the two girls ——'

Mayne's sentence did not sound quite finished. Mrs. Wastel said, 'That will be eight, with Jones ; for you must needs take me as odd old woman, unless you propose Lady Somers.'

'Fancy her in the break—like a peacock in a higgler's basket! I shall not want Jones : Tim can open the gates. Then we can have Cordelia ; she is better company than Jones.'

Mrs. Wastel paused, considering. There had been a good deal of Cordelia lately, except during the fortnight of Mayne's absence ; that might be accidental—but then it might not. Lettice spoke quickly. 'Yes, let us have Cordelia ; it will do her good.'

'I thought Miss Spenser was the agent for doing her good,' said Mrs. Wastel.

'She will be all day away from Maybury, and——'

Here Mrs. Wastel was called away, saying, as she left the room, ' Ask her, if you like.'

'Go on, Lettice,' said Mayne.

'About Cordelia? I think there is something odd about her.'

'There was a good deal. I thought the

poor thing was being shaped to pattern now.'

'This is different. I think she is going to take up some religious turn.'

'There are people who think that a good thing.'

'Of course, Mayne; you know what I mean. Cordelia is not natural over it; she is so vehement and furious, taking quite a craze.'

'A little enthusiasm is refreshing when it is not on too small a matter. Her subject is momentous enough. Do the parsons bear too hard on her?'

'She listens to no one but Philip, and is so excited over him; she is worse than the Maybury ladies; if she is not as absurd as Miss Peabody, she is more *tête montée*.'

'Don't speak French, unless you wish to show off. She might have a worse craze than a parsonic one, and Philip will do her nothing but good in the long run. She is of a different nature from you; she is not so *rangée*.

There, I can be as fine as you in the matter
of French! Get along, old girl, and don't shy
at shadows.'

Cordelia went to Sandbay, and on the box
of the break. Mrs. Wastel thought Mayne
would keep that seat for Caro Somers, a very
merry, spirited girl, and good-looking too.
When the time should come for Mrs. Wastel to
leave the Warren to a stepdaughter-in-law she
thought she could leave it for Caro Somers
with a very good grace. But surely a man
may do as he likes with his own box-seat,
particularly when he is driving from it himself.
Cordelia looked a credit to any one's break, and
she chattered all the way in her friendliest
fashion. Tim Somers was content to walk up
the hills with her. Fifteen miles of country,
chiefly fir plantations and open heathery common, lay between the Warren and the coast;
the hills were steep, the road sandy, and the
horses must be eased a little. Charlotte Somers
had lately engaged herself to a young barrister,

who must get a little further on in his profession before he could claim her. She liked
to stay with Mrs. Wastel in the carriage and
talk about him, while Caro walked with Mayne
by the horses' heads, discussing a litter of collie
puppies that were her uppermost delight at
present. Thus by hill and dale they came to
the last cliff overlooking Sandbay, halted
to combine the best point of view with due
attention to the luncheon-basket, and so down
into the pretty watering-place, which had made
such an effort to be gay and festive that it was
more evident than usual that it was an extremely quiet place.

The regatta was not exciting, and there
was a slight mist over the sea, so that the
yacht races were for the most part invisible.
The spirits of the party were quite unimpaired
by this trifle. Mrs. Wastel went to see a
friend; the others strolled on the sands and
climbed over the rocks into the next bay, a
salt and solitary recess where their laughter

seemed out of place until some one proposed sea-songs. Charlotte led them, and they sang several together; then she sang alone the 'Sands of Dee.' Tim voted this too tragic, and asked Cordelia to sing. She declined entirely, and with some confusion which seemed out of place. Mayne guessed that she remembered with shame her Silverwood singing, and named a Neapolitan fisher song that he had heard since. She shook her head, and began the hymn for those at sea, 'Eternal Father'; the rest joined her, and it sounded sweet and solemn over the summer sea. More than one of the young people thought of 'perils on the sea' of this troublesome world, which as yet seemed blue and shining for all of them. Lettice could not have been one of these, for she said to Tim, as he helped her over the rocks on their way back, 'I could bear to be taken for cheap trippers, but to be thought a revival party is too much for my strength of mind.'

Before they left the town, Cordelia, with Jock and Caro, set off up the steep little main street of Sandbay in search of a shop where Jock said toffee was sold of a peculiar and excellent make. They found it, and laid in a good stock for use on the homeward journey. Jock, with his sticky parcel, was a step behind the girls, when, in leaving the shop, they met two gentlemen, in yachting dress, arm in arm, very jocose, and a little disposed to turn them off the narrow pavement. Caro went quietly past as if she saw not, and Jock from behind lifted up his ugly face with such an air that the heroes recollected themselves and were giving way, when one of them, who was the Hon. George Kingdon, recognised Cordelia.

'Hullo! Why, Corks, it's never you!'

Cordelia stopped short, looking at him bravely but with scarlet cheeks. 'How do you do?' she asked, faintly and incuriously, as, with a glance at her companions, he lifted his hat, a little too late for a perfect salute.

The Somerses went on a few steps, but Mr. Kingdon's companion leant against the bow-window of the toffee-shop and considered Cordelia at his ease.

'I hardly knew you myself, and I am sure your parent would not dream that this dignified young lady was his once-loved Corks.'

'Hush! Is he here?' Cordelia threw a wild glance around her as if she would run, could she but see a safe direction.

'Calm yourself. He is at Merle Hill, six good miles from here, laid up with some complaint that he does not give a name to, but which makes him short in the temper and the legs. What a brick you were, Corks, to send me that message! I roared over it at first, and then I thought it was a beastly shame to laugh.'

'It *was*! Good-bye.' But, quicker than she could fly, he seized her arm.

'Don't be silly; I am planning to go and see you on Monday, when I go through May-

bury. I shall call at your Cottage without
fail, unless you think it better to stroll down
to the station at four o'clock. You shall tell
me all about it, 'pon my word you shall—as
you promised, you know. Good-bye till
Monday.'

Cordelia twitched her elbow from his de-
taining hand and sped down the street to her
friends. 'A man I knew at Mentone,' she
explained airily, but they saw she panted and
her face still flamed. Jock turned off to help
Mayne with the horses, and Caro said to
Cordelia, 'Why do you blush so when you
meet any one? You turned scarlet when that
man spoke to you.'

'There was no reason, but I cannot help
it.'

'You must help it; you are not a ninny,
and need not look like one; besides, it makes
men think all sorts of things—that you think
too much of them.'

'The wretches. I think very little of this

one. I hate them when they think things, don't you?'

'I do; but they will, even the nice ones. A governess we once had showed me that it would not do to colour up and look as if some great thing were happening if a gentleman spoke to one unexpectedly. You know some girls are such fools, one would not care to be thought like them.'

'No one ever told me that kind of thing. You were all tremendously well brought up; at first I did not like you because of that, but now I see you are just as chummy as if you had not been brought up at all.'

Caro laughed. 'That is great praise, for you are the chummiest girl I know, and you were not three days in learning to like us.'

Cocktail and the Grey made light of eight persons in the cool of the evening, and trotted merrily when their heads were turned homewards. There was not much walking till they came to the last hill, then all the insides got down, leaving Mayne and Cordelia on their lofty seat.

'Tired, Cordie? You have not spoken for the last four miles.'

'I am not tired; but the sunset makes me think, or yearn, as Miss Carling would say,' she answered, turning her face toward the clear yellow light that shone behind the fir-trees on the hill to the left of them.

'You are new to thinking, and work too hard at it, child. Did you meet a friend in Sandbay?'

Her face changed suddenly; she had not been thinking of George Kingdon, though a little time before she was rejoicing and trembling over her narrow escape, saying to herself, 'I should have to run away and hide for shame if these dear people knew that I was called Corks.' As a matter of fact, Jock had heard perfectly, and told Mayne, who watched her as she answered, 'Yes. How did you know?'

'Two fellows came into the inn-yard as the

horses were put to. One I know to be about the worst bargain in the county, Mostin of Merle Hill, a man I do not care to speak to; all the decent fellows about here have cut him. Somers did not even know him by sight. He said the other man had been speaking to you.'

'Yes, it is George Kingdon, Lord Rowe's son.'

'He is a very chickaleery-looking chap, and keeps poor company. I should think he would be the only person likely to complain if you dropped him, Cordie.'

'Suppose it had been my father! He is staying at Merle Hill, and is as chickaleery-looking as George. You have never seen my awful dad.'

Mayne was taken aback, and did not know how to proceed with his lecture. Her father!

'It would be rather sneakish to drop George, don't you think? He has been very good to me for two winters, when no one else was; he often took me for a walk at Mentone;

and once he went without his dinner and
walked four miles to get me out of a
hobble.'

'What could you have been doing to want
such a haul as that?'

'If you had asked me when I first came
here I should have told you—not now. Do
you know, I am a sneak, for if I had seen
George before he saw me I should have run—
down that queer little street, right into the sea!
When he was talking to me, with that man
standing by sneering, I was quite frightened
to think that I belong to them.'

'Belong to them! Cordelia!'

'Yes; they are my father's friends, Sophy's
too. We Ashbys are that sort of people—just
that, Mayne.'

'Nonsense ; no one can be said to belong to
their father's acquaintance ; and as to your
father'—here honest Mayne felt himself in
difficulties—'well, he is your father, and you
must make the best of him.'

'So every one says. No one has told me how, yet.'

' As to his friends, if they are of Mostin's stamp—good heavens ! the less you see of them the better. Besides, you belong, as you call it, to your mother's people as well.'

' If I could only belong to them !—really, always ! '

' You shall if you choose,' said Mayne, who could only himself be said to belong to them by a stretch of courtesy.

Here the top of the hill became obvious, even to the horses, and the others were heard lamenting that they had not been taken up a quarter of a mile past.

The next Sunday Mr. Odiarne preached a mighty sermon on the power of a holy life over the lives of others; without such a life no words, no works, will avail to benefit them ; but with it the humblest may win his thousands. There is not in the world so great a power, so strong an influence, as is exerted by such a life—far greater, stronger, and more widely reaching than an evil life ; for 'greater is He that is for us than he that is against us.' It must be a life the inner springs of which are hid with Christ in God ; from that it follows that it is pure, saintly, disciplined : that it is full of lovingkindness and humility, of patience, hope, and good deeds. It must be a life of constant and entire self-sacrifice, often one of suffering ; though the suffering and the sacrifice may be hidden from the public eye, and not to be measured by the popular estimate. Such a life will deepen and brighten as it runs its course, till it lends glory to the countenance and power to the speech ; till the face shines like Stephen's, and the voice pleads like Paul's. Through all its years, and often long after death, such a life will draw up, strengthen, inspire, and sustain other lives that more or less nearly touch it, and is one of God's great instruments of conversion. The power of such lives can be traced in all history, is felt in all experiences, the strongest, sweetest, most abiding influence that man can bring to bear on his fellow-man, the infinite, the immeasurable, the eternal power of a holy life.

That day Mr. Merridew was at Ivy Cottage; he had been in the parish church in the morning.

'Miss Hooper, who did you think of most when the Vicar was preaching this morning?' he asked.

'Of those who were dead before you were born; of my mother chiefly, she answered well to that description. It is strange, but Cordelia, her great-granddaughter, sometimes brings her to my mind.'

'And you, Miss Ashby?' he asked, looking a little disappointed.

'I thought a little of dear Sœur Lucie, and of an old woman I used to know, but most of Mr. Odiarne himself.'

'That is right!' said the curate, with restored radiance. 'I thought every one must be thinking of him, and he would be so astonished to hear that any one did.'

'I did not forget him, Mr. Merridew ; but— thank God for them—I have known many such lives, and have seen them finish their course,' said Aunt Susan, with feeling, yet a little severely.

'I have never seen any one like him. I do not see how any one could be like him !' said Cordelia, hotly.

'Such men are always rare, but the holy lives he speaks of are not so very uncommon —as Elijah found. They are the salt of the earth, and I believe there is always salt enough to keep even times like these sweet. You must think so, too, or you will lose heart,' said the old lady to Mr. Merridew.

'I do believe it, though I have been lately passing through the stage of believing every one bad, because I could no longer believe every one good.'

'Did you ever do that ? ' said Cordelia,

surprised that even this young parson could ever have taken so fresh a view, while her aunt was surprised that he could have advanced beyond it.

'It is the best belief to be brought up in, I think, that "the wicked man" is a vague abstraction heard of chiefly in church; but it is sore work coming out of it. The Vicar keeps up one's heart, however. I thought he was very fine to-day. When he warms up and gets that exalted spiritual look, even his appearance is very striking.'

'I think he is always beautiful to look at— like the saints in the windows,' said Cordelia, with quiet force.

'You young people think so much of looks,' said Aunt Susan.

'Would you like the Vicar as well if he were very fat and had a purple face?' asked Mr. Merridew, laughing, as he prepared to go. 'Miss Ashby, would you not like to go to the Brook Street schoolroom this evening? I

think the Vicar will be there,' he added, as
Cordelia began to decline.

' Oh, Aunt Susan ! may I ? '

' My dear, I do not think you ought to be
in Brook Street so late in the evening. Well,
see if French will go with you.'

This was an enormous concession for Aunt
Susan, who disliked that even the old maids
should go to evening services; that young
women should stay at home and read their
Bibles after dark was her theory, but the spirit
of the times was too strong for her in the
matter of practice.

Mr. Odiarne, pursuing the thoughts of his
morning sermon, spoke in the same spirit,
but in different form, to the simple folk who
gathered in the Brook Street schoolroom. He
told them that they ought to help each other
along the narrow way, and he told them how
to do it.

One consequence of his day's preaching was
that Cordelia decided that it was her duty to

take the present opportunity of influencing George Kingdon. 'I must meet him,' she thought, ' or else get out of the way altogether. It will not do to let him come swinging up the garden, and perhaps call out " Corks " at the window. Besides, I cannot possibly speak seriously to him with Aunt Susan looking on.'

CHAPTER XV.

MOTIVE POWERS.

And young and kind, and royally blind,
Forth she stepped from her palace door.
              E. B. Browning.

On Monday afternoon, a little past four o'clock, Mr. Odiarne and Mayne Wastel were walking towards Maybury down the hill by Ivy Cottage. All was silent in the hot garden, and the road too was nearly as deserted. Suddenly, thirty yards ahead of them, Cordelia Ashby dropped out of the yew-tree on to the turf border of the road. She never looked in their direction, but walked quickly towards the town. The two men laughed.

'I thought she had given that up,' said Mayne.

'And I begged her not to do it; so much for one's counsel,' answered Mr. Odiarne.

'By Jove! look there!' This was drawn from Mayne at the sight of George Kingdon, who at that moment met Cordelia. She must have seen him from the yew-tree. They slackened their pace, expecting the pair to turn; but Cordelia, slipping her arm through Mr. Kingdon's, turned him abruptly down a little lane that led from the high road past the end of Miss Hooper's garden. When they crossed the end of the lane Cordelia and her friend were going towards the fields; she had dropped his arm, but was talking eagerly to him.

'Who is it, Mayne? Any one you know?'

'He is the Hon. George Kingdon—some precious scamp of her father's delectable circle of acquaintance. One of the Merle Hill set; old Ashby is there now.'

'And what of this proceeding?'

'I don't understand it. She met the fellow for a few minutes in the street at Sandbay last week, but the monkey told me—I mean I

warned her that he was not the best of company, and she expressed some dread of him,
saying she would gladly not have spoken to
him ; this is the last thing I expected.' Mayne
looked very much vexed, and Mr. Odiarne
hardly less so and much more severe.

'This is an arranged meeting. It will be
heart-breaking to Miss Hooper to find herself
so grossly deceived.'

' Perhaps my people had better see to
it,' said Mayne, regretfully. ' Unless you will
speak to her yourself, Philip. I do not like the
idea of springing a mine on her ; but this must
be stopped.'

' In any case I must speak to her ; she is
not only deceiving her aunt, but playing the
hypocrite in a way I cannot permit.'

' She would not do that ; I am sure she
speaks the truth. Perhaps this fellow has some
hold on her ; if so he must be kicked. She
did say he got her out of some scrape at Mentone. I can credit a man with any villainy

who stays at Merle Hill, but not so easily believe she is playing us all false.'

'If you knew what tricks our pupil-teachers and other picked girls will sometimes play us, you might not be so confiding. I always turn them over to Knox, who is impervious to all wiles and wheedles. I wish I had left this one to him; but she belongs to you all in a way, and Lettice answered for her; I thought these girls understood one another. I am very much disappointed here, for I believed in this child's sincerity and single-mindedness,' growled the Vicar.'

'Get a wife, Philip. Perhaps if you understood one good woman you might find a clue to the rest.'

'I should be stone-blind then, instead of only one-eyed. I doubt if a woman can be said to be proved till she is as old as Aunt Susan. If there were not a man like Knox here and there to tackle them, I could wish that women had no souls.'

'There's a sentiment for a popular preacher! Why, Philip, that minx Cordelia cried a pailful on Sunday while you were preaching, and Lettice said she went with Merridew to hear you again in Brook Street.'

'I may forgive her this prank, on her submission; but if she makes a fool of Merridew I won't, so there.'

'As you saw her just now, I leave this to you, for I suppose she must have her bad quarter of an hour over it, poor girl.'

'Certainly she must; and the more I like her the less she must be spared.'

A few days passed before Mr. Odiarne was able to go to Ivy Cottage. His distaste for his errand did not make him find the opportunity any faster, in which he differed from Mr. Knox, who would have had it out at once. Cordelia was sitting in the verandah; the moment she saw the broad hat over the shrubs she ran down to meet the wearer, with a very downcast and troubled face.

' I want so much to see you ; can you spare
me a little of the precious time in the garden
before you go to Aunt Susan ? '

' It is you that I come to see to-day,' said
the Vicar, wondering if Mayne had been before-
hand with him.

' I have not really read the chapters you
marked for me, nor got on with this book at
all, for I can think of nothing but the dreadful
mess I have got into. You will be very angry.'

' Not if you tell me all the truth about it.'

' All the truth ! Mr. Odiarne, I should
despise my very self if I told anything but the
truth to you. I don't often tell a lie, never on
purpose, I always thought it sneaking ; but I
should be wicked indeed if I told anything but
the very truth to you.'

' To me ! I have told you before that you
consider too much what I may personally think ;
you trust me to teach you aright, and that is
enough. You must try to act on the principles
I show you; truth is one of the first, and

because both God and man require it of you in all things you must tell it now, not because you are talking to me.'

The tone was far gentler than the words; Cordelia answered with a look of perfect trust, the respect and affection that prompted it were plain enough, but it was doubtful if she took in the force of the appeal to general principles as well as if it had been made by Mr. Knox or Aunt Susan.

'It was a man I met at Sandbay, a friend of mine at Mentone. Mayne told me he was no good at all. I know that; all the men we knew there were a shady set; but George Kingdon was different—not at all a good man, but not a bad fellow, you know.'

Mr. Odiarne signified his comprehension of this delicate distinction.

'He looked horrid at Sandbay, not nice at all; but he said he was coming here, and wanted me to tell him about you, and all you have taught me. I promised long ago that I would tell him as soon as I found any very good person to teach me. He used to be jolly and friendly to me when no one else was, and I longed so much—so very much—to tell him some of the beautiful things you have told me, and say in your sermons, and what it is to be good. I think George might be good if he made up his mind, though all our people would scream with laughter at the idea of it; but I know George better than a good many of them—or I thought I did. He was so disagreeable at Sandbay, and Mayne thought I ought to cut him, so that I was in a great puzzle about it for a day or two, and could not tell if I would or I would not; but you made up my mind on Sunday. I was sure it would be right to use my influence and to show him the beauty of holiness; you said so?'

'Not quite. Once I told you a much easier thing—not to jump out of that tree.'

'So you did; but I thought it would not do to think of manners when it was a question of a person's soul, and I knew George would not precisely suit Aunt Susan, so I stopped him and took him down Crookett's Lane. I spoke very seriously to him, the very best I knew; all I could think of that I had heard from you, and things Mrs. Wastel had said, and—but——' Here Cordelia got into difficulties, she grew hot and shy, and sobs came into her voice. It was too much to say face to face sitting there on the garden bench. Mr. Odiarne made her pace along the rose walk by his side, and with her face meekly drooped out of sight by his elbow, she struggled on.

'He did not take it rightly at all; he does not really care. He laughed and said dreadful things, going on in the old horrid fashion that I never thought funny even then, but now it hurts me—and he said things that made me ashamed, about you. I need not tell them, need I?'

'No; and you need not mind them, either; do not let them trouble you in the

least. Is there any more that you must tell
me?'

'Only just the worst. He thought I was
not in earnest, and only wanted to meet him—
him—as if—I cared for him—just foolishly.
Oh, Mr. Odiarne! I have made him hate goodness instead of loving it, and despise me; what
ought I to have said?'

'Nothing at all. But tell me the end of
your interview.'

'When I found he only wanted to talk
nonsense, as if I were Sophy and cared for
that sort of thing. I jumped down that bank at
the turn of the lane, where it is wet, and ran
across the long field to the end of the garden.
I got up the sunk fence into the orchard, and
when I looked back he was lighting a cigar
and prospecting for the road to the station. If
he found the foot-bridge, he would be in time
for his train.'

Mr. Odiarne was moved to laughter, and
guilty of a wish to impart these confidences to

Mayne; but even this informal confession must be sacred, and as for the laughter, Cordelia's real distress quenched that desire. He said gravely, 'So you have been casting your pearls before swine.'

'Swine! Oh, is not that rough on poor George?'

'They are not my words; they were spoken to those who, like you, had but lately found their pearls. You are but a child, Cordelia, when you rashly show your treasures to the first comer. And then you are so new a learner, do you think you are fit to teach?'

This rebuke went home, and Mr. Odiarne went on to say more than can be written down here, ending with, 'Do not be discouraged. When you are ready to teach others you will find work ready to your hand, and when you make your next experiment let it be with a more suitable person than a fast young man.'

'I can never speak to him again after the things he said. Once he was very kind to me when I got into a scrape, almost as kind as you are now.'

A question as to the nature and extent of her obligations brought out the story of Cordelia's expedition to Monte Carlo. She was ashamed of it, but not so much so as of her recent failure. Full of pity for the neglected girl, and unwilling to complicate her duties for the future, Mr. Odiarne made very little remark on her story; but in speaking of the gambling he said, 'If you are living near that place again, I would advise you not to go there unless it be an actual matter of obedience to your father; and surely you need not play again.'

'Never, I promise you. But the money? I spent it all, and the frocks are worn out.'

'Well, you can make it up in course of time by small self-denials, and that will make it a fit offering when you can see your way to its doing good. Take care that it is yourself that you deny, not other people; and if you

are some time in saving this sum it will keep
you the longer in mind of this talk, among
other things. The money is a trifle. I want
you to do something that will cost you more.
I will only point it out, and you can do it of
your own free-will. I shall not ask if it has
been done. It is that you should tell all this
to Mrs. Wastel. Is that hard?'

'Yes.'

'But you love her?'

'Oh, yes! She is the dearest dear!'

'And you have told me.'

'That is different, quite!'

'It would distress Aunt Susan, and to no
good purpose. She is a generation further
from you than your cousin, and she is unused
to modern ways and modern forms of evil.
Do you know, she was much in my mind in
my sermons the other day. I have known
many conspicuous saints, such as those whose
names illumine the ages all along; but there
are many more who are rarely spoken of, never

written of, whose holy lives are of scarcely less value. Hers is one of them. I am never with her without feeling its power. I cannot have that pleasure to-day, for I have spent my time on you.'

Cordelia executed herself bravely in the matter of confession to Mrs. Wastel, and she had her reward, not only in a taste of the mother-love that could never be fully hers, but in a great opening out, under her gentle counsels, of the perfumed flower of woman-hood, the outer leaves of which George Kingdon had so rudely brushed ; the bud had hitherto been folded too tightly for either softness or sweetness, there was only a flush of the brighter tones of colour and the promise of future expansion. In the succeeding weeks she made rapid progress in outward things, and even Mayne was willing to allow that there might be a happy medium between a fair barbarian and a conventional young lady.

' And I think that we may consider her as

a proof that love, a lover's love, is not the only civiliser,' said Mrs. Wastel.

'I know you think that although love in the Revised Version sense is the one means of good, yet that the power of romantic love is much exaggerated,' said Mayne.

'The exaggeration lies in its being repre-sented as the only power; the poets and novelists do this very often for art purposes, and in all the fair realm of romance Love is the rightful king, as Beauty is crowned queen; but even in the lives of the young and fair there are other forces than love and other kingdoms than romance, and they ought to be taken into account. The family and filial love that goes for so much with most girls has been absent from hers till now, and she is enjoying it with all the more zest that it has not come to her naturally and insen-sibly.'

' She is not very romantic,' said Mayne.

' Do you think not? She lives entirely in

her feelings,' observed Lettice, who had not yet spoken, contrary to her custom. 'Something is improving her very much.'

'Yes,' answered Mrs. Wastel. 'I think it is grace—not manner, nor manners only, though it shows so much in that way—but Grace, with a capital. She is striving after goodness with all her heart, and it softens and beautifies her whole character from the inside. I am so glad we persevered with her, and were not disgusted at first. It will be a great healing of an old sorrow for us elders if Rosina's daughter should turn out well.'

'It will be a great credit to some people if Colonel Ashby's daughter should turn out well; but you must work upon her for a considerable time longer,' said Mayne, who was a little sore that he had never fully fathomed the George Kingdon episode. Philip told him it was all right—Cordelia was not much to blame; and his stepmother had given him the same unsatisfactory assurance. Lettice, his usual resort, was unavailable, for he would not betray Cordelia to her unbiassed judgments.

When they were alone Lettice said to her mother, 'You will think I am a vixen; but I cannot take quite the same view of Cordelia as you do. I am not so sure about the power that is moving her.'

'Surely you do not think she is deceiving us?'

'Oh, no! But I think she is deceiving herself. I am sure she is trying honestly to be good; but she is too new at it, and floundering about far too awkwardly among her new motives for her goodness to have any beautifying effect just yet. It is something else.'

'Oh, Lettice! do you mean Mayne? I do not want to be a foolish old hen, but I have watched them; she treats him exactly as if it were you—rather too much like you sometimes; but it is a fault on the right side. Then her connections are so doubtful, and Mayne is so particular.'

'Mayne is very like other young men; but I was not thinking of him.'

'Of Jock Somers?' asked Mrs. Wastel, much relieved, though whether Lady Somers would have shared her relief is at least doubtful.

'Philip taught me, as he does Cordelia; and I am for ever grateful, and think him the best of men, and the first of cousins; but do you think I ever made such a fuss about him as Cordelia does?'

'Oh! Let me have time to take this in— I do not like the suggestion at all. You cannot surely think her so base, so wicked, as to make her Christian training a cover for ——. Oh, Lettice! It is too bad to contemplate!'

'No, no! She is quite sincere; but she is thinking, moving, breathing, in an atmosphere of Philip. He is more like an idol than a saint to her, she has so glorified him. She has an ascetic turn on now, and will not eat anything she likes, so that the old maids are distracted,

and Aunt Susan has hunted out a family recipe
for spring medicine ; Cordie would have taken
it because it is so nasty, only it is September,
and French thinks it might not suit the time of
year.   She has bought a pair of cotton gloves,
baggy at the thumbs, and when I declined to
be seen with them, she said she would buy
another pair, for Mr. Odiarne told her to deny
herself, not other people ; I wish she had stuck
to the cottons, it would have been more natural.'

Mrs. Wastel laughed.   'You frightened
me at first, but this only shows a youthful
enthusiasm ;   Philip   is   the   last   man   to
encourage it.'

'He is the last man to see it.   He raises
his lofty head, and fixes his far-seeing eyes on
distant realms of bliss, and will never notice
that a little nincompoop like Cordie is making
a fool of herself under his feet.'

'Well, my dear, you would not wish him
to be always on the look-out for little nincom-
poops.'

'No, and I have no objection to Miss Peabody and Mrs. Bloxer talking about the dear Vicar, and the edification of a conversation with him at the street-corner about the coal club, but I do not like it to be our cousin.'

'It will be better to take no notice, it is only a passing absurdity. There was a very stirring and popular preacher in London when I was young, about whom I and my friends made great geese of ourselves; but it evaporated in good time, and I, for one, gained much solid good as a residue when the effervescence was past.'

END OF THE FIRST VOLUME.

LONDON : PRINTED BY
SPOTTISWOODE AND CO., NEW-STREET SQUARE
AND PARLIAMENT STREET

www.ingramcontent.com/pod-product-compliance
Lightning Source LLC
Chambersburg PA
CBHW021045030726
47496CB00006B/1690